HEAVY MEDDLE MAGIC

OWL STAR WITCH MYSTERIES BOOK 4

LEANNE LEEDS

Heavy Meddle Magic
Paperback ISBN: 978-1-950505-55-5
Published by Badchen Publishing
14125 W State Highway 29
Suite B-203 119
Liberty Hill, TX 78642 USA

For permissions contact: info@badchenpublishing.com

CONTENTS

HEAVY MEDDLE MAGIC

CHAPTER ONE

"*L*ook, it's not like I have an issue with your job," Jason said as his steady, rhythmic steps slowed to a stop. "I might find it difficult to work for the police considering the issues I see on the news every day, and I just wondered how you felt about it. That's all."

It was early in the morning, and Jason Bishop —my running partner—brought up the socio-economic issues plaguing modern policing while we slowed to stretch halfway through our morning run. Fortunately, my job as a psychic consultant for the Forkbridge Police Department left me relatively insulated from the problems on the news every day, and I wasn't thrilled he'd brought the subject up.

Since I was a psychic and not a cop, who cares what I think, anyway. Right?

Besides, I worked in Forkbridge, Florida. Our small Southern town between Orlando and the coast cared little about anything other than traffic and tourists. Nothing ever happened here.

Well, I mean…except for when it did.

I raised my eyebrow at Jason while I stretched and wondered what on earth made him strike up this conversation now. He'd never spoken about anything like this before, and I'd never given him the impression that anyone should approach me about much of anything before my coffee.

"Look, Jason, I come out here and run in the morning so I can think about my day. Not contemplate the state of the world, and my possible contribution to its negatives solely through my association with an organization that may—or may not—have systemic societal issues." I took a deep drink from my water bottle, capped it, and shoved it back on my belt. "Besides, don't you work for the school district that just got busted for passing students that couldn't read?"

"The district, not me. And whatever they do, I still feel like I'm contributing to the betterment of society," he replied. "Next generation and all that. Or I'm trying, at least. There's a difference between working for the police department and working for the school district, you know."

Pass judgment much?

I walked over to a park bench a few yards away and sat down. The contrast between the heat of my body through my soaked shirt and the cool air of the morning chilled me. "I guess that's true. Yeah, you're absolutely right." I could hear the snotty condescension in my own voice, but he'd annoyed me, and I didn't rein it in.

"I am?" he asked, surprised.

"Absolutely. You approach your job from the mindset that you can impact the growth of young minds in a positive way. I just keep those young minds from getting splattered on the street by sociopaths. You're right. You're much more important than I am. Much more virtuous. Clearly." I looked up. "We good now?"

I grabbed my sweat towel from my hip and wiped my face as Jason caught up to me and sat down. The bench was old and faded but still used. It sheltered in the shadows of a tree above it, the scarred trunk and branches stirring in the slight breeze.

"Look, I didn't mean it like that. I'm sorry," he said, trying to backpedal. "I—"

"Just stop talking, dude."

He did, and an uncomfortable silence stretched between us.

After a minute, I sighed. "Look, I think about impact and contribution in my own way, but I don't think about it at all while I'm running. And not first thing in the morning. I just need some quiet time to myself where I can clean my head of cobwebs and get ready for work."

He looked at me, surprised. "Not at all?"

"No. I don't think about the existence of evil in the world first thing in the morning. And I sure as heck don't want to start discussing how much of it I should be held personally accountable for while drenched in sweat and before coffee," I said. I was sarcastic, but Jason's face was so earnest it made me feel bad. "Look, I'm not mad. But I'm also just not interested."

Jason tilted his head to the side, eyes narrowed. Then, eager to move past his mistake, he nodded with a smile. "Okay, sure. Sorry about that. It just popped in there. I'll avoid current events discussions before your coffee."

"I'd appreciate it. That type of discussion is for nighttime. Preferably, with a drink in my hand," I told him and leaned forward to get up. I heard the roar of a siren in the distance, then the blare of a horn, and chuckled, changing the subject. "People can't even wait until the sun's up some days."

"Well, maybe we could meet for dinner or drinks to—"

Jason stopped mid-sentence and stared over my shoulder. His eyes got wide, and his mouth dropped open. "What the…"

I turned to look behind me just in time to see a large owl swooping toward us. The mass of its body made an audible swooshing noise the closer it got, like the gust of wind before a storm.

"Duck!" I yelled.

"No, owl!" Archie, my magical divine owl, screeched as he flew straight into Jason's face. "I don't look anything like a freaking duck!"

"Ow! What the hell? Why did it do that? Ow! Ow! Ow!" Jason yelled, trying to knock the bird off his face with the flats of his hands—and I have to admit that for a moment, I found Jason's unwillingness to harm the psychotic, murderous raptor rather sweet. Especially since the force of Archie hitting Jason's face had knocked him off the park bench and onto the grass.

I ran over to the flailing teacher, helped him

up, and pulled the owl off his head. Then with a glare, I tossed Archie on the ground.

Archie flapped around for a few moments before finding his bearings and stretching out his massive wings. "There! I kept him from asking you out on a date," Archie called up to me. "You owe me!"

"You're out of your mind, bird!" I told the owl. In response, he took off into the air and hovered for a moment, silently, his wings moving slowly. "Shoo, random owl I don't know!"

"I bet you refusing his question would have been more violent, you frigid thirty-something," the owl responded, his head tilting. "I was just trying to head that off. Someday you may want to actually date the hot dude as opposed to just outright refusing every male suitor that doesn't have the brains to realize you're going to rip them to shreds verbally for suggesting drinks."

I...did not do that.

Archie launched himself, gliding gracefully through the air until he settled on a nearby tree. Then, with a step to the right, the owl camouflaged himself so he was nearly invisible. "We can talk about it at home!"

I glared once more and turned back toward Jason. "Are you okay?" I asked.

Jason squatted in the grass, holding his face, a few brown feathers in his hand. He was baffled, but his eyes were fixed on me. "He actually didn't hurt me at all. I'm fine. Just a little surprised, that's all."

"You and me both," I murmured.

I WENT HOME, and my sister Ami poured me some coffee. "Althea and Ayla"—our other two sisters —"are still asleep." She frowned as she caught sight of the smudged mud on my uniform. "What happened to you? You look like you wrestled an alligator. There's a twig in your hair." She pointed toward my temple.

I reached up and yanked it out. "Archie came on the run. Then he flew into Jason's face. Like, full owl speed ahead. Where's Mom and Aunt Gwennie?"

"In the root cellar checking on the Stinkhorn mushrooms." Suddenly, her eyes grew wide as she handed me the mug. "Wait a minute. Archie did what?"

"Attacked Jason. Flew into his face while we were talking."

"But why?" Ami asked.

I shook my head. "I don't know. It was some weird thing about not letting the 'hot dude' ask me out on a date or something. I don't think it made a whole lot of sense, to be honest," I replied.

Ami's eyebrows came together. "You know, Astra, maybe he was just trying to get to know you. Get an opinion on something important to him."

Archie had my sister wrapped around his razor-sharp talon in some ways. "That owl doesn't care about my opinion on anything."

Ami gave me a look somewhere between amusement and frustration. "Jason Bishop. I'm talking about Jason Bishop. You know, the cute guy you go running with practically every morning. You really aren't functional before coffee, are you?"

"No, and that's possible."

She nodded, then frowned. "Wait. What's possible?"

"That Jason was trying to get to know me better. Though I wouldn't know since my owl flew into his face before he could finish his sentence."

"Did you say yes?"

"To what?"

She sighed loudly. "Oh, my gosh, you're

unbelievable. When he asked you out, did you say yes?" Ami asked slowly as if she were talking to a child. "If Archie heard it, you must have, too."

"No. No, and no," I said. I walked across the kitchen to the television on the kitchen bar and switched on the morning news. "He didn't really ask me, though. He almost asked me. He tried to start a deep conversation with me when I was on my run and wanted to talk about his overall societal contribution. Or mine. Or something, I don't know." I took another sip of coffee and walked back toward the counter to pour as much sugar into it as I thought I could get away with. "Then he suggested we talk about it at night. Or I made a flippant comment, and he almost did. Archie overheard that and decided it was his sacred duty to save me from the question."

"That bird seems to think he has a lot of sacred duties," Ami chuckled.

"At least he stopped eating the bunnies in the backyard," I pointed out.

"That's only because Althea helped me enchant them to smell like peppermint and taste like cayenne pepper," my sister reminded me. "Though I don't think he ever got past the candy cane scent to find out the second part."

I sat down on a stool, and we watched the news together.

An overly cheerful blond reporter assured everyone the day would be sunny and warm with a chance of thunderstorms in the afternoon. Considering this was central Florida, I wasn't sure how sunny, warm, and a chance of afternoon thunderstorms qualified as news—since that was more or less every day—but apparently?

It did.

"As the famous enclave of Cassandra gets ready for its annual Halloween festival this weekend, tragedy struck the town. Mayor Lillian Thornton barely escaped a two-alarm fire last night as her ancestral home, Thornton House, went up in flames. Despite the emergency, she assured our reporter John Trainer the full weekend's activities will go on as planned. From the spiritual to the macabre, spooks and psychics alike will take to the streets to celebrate this once-a-year special event. John Trainer, on location, has more. John?"

The bottle blond tossed to a man with blindingly white teeth and a cheery smile. I wouldn't think you'd want to look cheerful in front of the smoldering ruin of someone's home but apparently?

You did.

"Ugh," Ami said, lowering the volume. "Don't let Mom hear about that. She'll start her complaining early. I was hoping to postpone it until Halloween night."

I frowned. "What, she has a problem with the festival? Why?"

"Don't tell me your thirteen years in the military made you forget about Mom's Halloween prejudice. She still thinks the Europeans stole the idea of Halloween from Anthesteria," Ami told me with an eye roll. "And she still complains about it every single year. You could set the wheel of the year by it."

Oh, right.

I did almost forget about that.

You probably have no idea what we're talking about.

So, it's a common misconception that all paranormals love Halloween—that isn't the case. Not by a long shot. My family's made up of Hellenic witches. (Which makes sense considering my mother is the goddess Athena's high priestess. Like, the only one. Kind of like a Hellenic witchy pope.) So, we celebrate ancient Greek holidays, not those with Celtic origins.

Anthesteria was a time when the souls of the

dead were temporarily released from Hades. The myth proclaims they were led right up to our plane of reality by Dionysus himself.

Dead spirits, frolicking in the land of the living...

Sounding familiar?

So, obviously, my mother believes Anthesteria—which takes place for three days in the month of Anthesterion—was the actual Halloween. Or that the Celts ripped off the Greeks to start Samhain (which became Halloween eventually).

Anthesteria was not in October, it had nothing to do with candy, and no one painted themselves green. It was around the time of the January or February full moon. I think.

Anyway.

Because of this perceived slight against the Greek gods, my mother didn't acknowledge Halloween and refused to participate in any festivities related to it. She even shut the porch light off so no children would mistake us for people with candy.

Odd for a family that owned a witch shop, right?

"Did they celebrate Halloween in Paranormopolis?" Ami asked.

I nodded yes. "They didn't celebrate Anthesteria, that's for sure."

I finished my coffee and watched the silent screen flicker images of Lillian Thornton's burned-out home in Cassandra. The lawn and front porch were black, and a sizable portion of the roof collapsed into a charred mess on the lawn on top of the remains of Lillian's vegetable garden. Yet, none of the destruction could wipe the smile from the face of the jaunty reporter.

Forkbridge, the town I lived in, was right next to the small village of Cassandra. We were slightly bigger than they were, but not by much. They were slightly more psychic than we were— Forkbridge just had us, a family of female witches and a witch shop. Cassandra had spiritualists and ghosts in almost every house in the town.

"You would think with as many ghosts as visit those people," I told Ami, hitching my chin toward the television, "that it would be impossible for a house to burn down. Wouldn't the spirits warn them?"

Spiritualists primarily spoke to the dead on behalf of the living. Because of their talent, and because so many people with that talent lived in Cassandra? The place was filled to the brim with dead people.

Ghosts, I mean.

Not, like zombies.

"That would be a better question for Mom or Ayla," Ami said between bites of a bagel. "I don't know much about what ghosts are actually interested in or not interested in. Like, would they alert the folks in Cassandra?" She shrugged. "Maybe they wouldn't interfere."

"Ghosts choosing not to interfere? Hasn't been my experience." I clicked the remote control, and the television flashed off. "I'm going to run upstairs and take a shower. You work at the shop today?"

Ami nodded. "Althea was up late working on some potion, so she asked me to take the morning shift."

"Is that what that smell was?" I made a face.

"I thought that smell was you," Ami teased and then stuck out her tongue. "Use the extra strength lavender soap. Or maybe go all the way up to the Eucalyptus one today."

"Rude," I told her and went up the stairs toward the bathroom.

I HAD to admit that I was grateful to live with five other witches—even if those witches were my annoying family, especially at moments like this. Confronting a wall of magical soaps within the walk-in shower, I have to admit this would be the envy of any Fifth Avenue spa.

After a few missteps with Althea's creative naming—Ayla turned blue after using "tranquil ocean blue" soap—my sister had taken to labeling our personal soaps so no one could misinterpret their effects. So I grabbed the bar marked "Sunny and Good and Happy Day" and breathed in the scent of lemongrass. The soap was smooth yet soft as a cloud, and the lather tingled with magic.

I'd been back at the police department for a couple of months without incident (and with a paycheck, thank goodness). Now that Captain Harmon knew about paranormals—or, to be more specific, I knew that Captain Harmon knew about paranormals—things had settled into a comfortable "don't ask, don't tell" scenario.

He knew.

We knew he knew.

Mostly, we just avoided talking about it.

Harmon redirected assignments that might involve paranormals toward Emma and me, which was good. It kept other officers from walking into something they didn't understand. With each case we handled, the more secure I felt about my job, and the less I worried about my paycheck disappearing.

I know, I know. I keep bringing up money.

My bank account had reflected what I'd lost when the new paranormal government fired the entire military, and I was grateful to have an independent source of money. Especially since the promised pension for all my years of service was still stuck in some committee at Paranormopolis.

I appreciated my mother's help, but at thirty-three years old? I was eager to get back out on my own again. I missed my independence, and I wasn't thrilled to be living in an attic where everyone in the house heard my comings and goings.

Sorry. My mind wandered. Where was I?

Oh, right.

Anyway, the other detectives and officers at the station had no knowledge of paranormals at all. They just knew that when a Forkbridge citizen called in something weird, it was best to just toss it to Detective Sullivan and her psychic gal pal.

That would be me.

I'm the psychic gal pal.

And since Emma's brother, Rex, opened up his vampire-themed dance club (and secret vampire B&B) just off the highway? Well, there was always another call or report of strange sightings or strange undercurrents of magic.

The speaker rang in the bathroom. "Alexa, answer the phone." I heard a click. "Hello?" I called over the sound of the water.

"Getting a late start this morning, are we?" Emma asked through the tinny Bluetooth speaker. "Or did you finally run off with Jason Bishop for some real recreational activity?"

I frowned. "I told you, we're just running partners."

"You guys run together almost every single day," Emma said, echoing Ami's observation a half an hour ago. "I can't believe he hasn't asked you out yet."

"I'm just running with Jason Bishop, not running off with him."

Her voice grew louder. "I mean, for goodness sake, Astra, he's hot...and he's a teacher, so you know he likes kids. So you could do worse."

"I already have a man in my life, Emma. Just because he's an owl doesn't make him any less of an annoying male to deal with."

I heard a knock on the door.

"I heard the knock. Hurry up and get down to the station. I'm already hearing the captain wants to talk to us," Emma said quickly. "He looks freaked out about something."

"I'll be out the door in ten and at the station in about thirty," I told her. Emma said she'd see me then and signed off.

The knocking became louder.

"Just a minute," I yelled, stepping out of the shower and grabbing a towel. I wrapped it around myself and threw the door open. My thirteen-year-old sister was glaring at me.

"If you get assigned the case about the house burning down and stuff in Cassandra? You better come back here and get me," she said with an indignant huff. Ayla's eyes were cold as an arctic lake, her mouth as thin as a knife's edge. She crossed her arms. "You haven't taken me on a case in months, and this one? This one is, like, made for me!"

"I work for the police department in Forkbridge, Ayla. Cassandra's a different police force. So we won't have anything to do with that fire."

My little sister rolled her eyes. "Oh, please. They'll totally call you. The house is haunted, and all those ghosts coming and going? I could interview everybody!" Her jaw was clenched in a misaligned sneer that made her look even younger than her thirteen years. "And there was a murder victim found in the yard once years ago, who used to live there when it was a hotel! And the fire? It maybe wasn't even fire. It could have been a magic attack—"

I took a deep breath and tried to remind myself that I was covered from head to toe in the sunny day I would absolutely have. "Like I said, I work for the police department in Forkbridge, Ayla." I climbed the stairs to my attic room, Ayla trailing behind me.

"But I want to work on a case!"

"And when I have a case that involves ghosts, Ayla, I will come to talk to you if you can help," I told the overly excited girl sternly. "Right now? I have to get to work, and I can't talk about this with you. I just don't have time."

She pouted. "You never take me on cases anymore."

I didn't technically take her on the first case she worked on, either. The stubborn little brat hid in the back of my Jeep. "Ayla, I—"

"No. Never mind. Forget it." My youngest sister whirled on her heel and stomped down the stairs loudly. When she got to the second floor, she shouted back up. "I don't even know why I ask. You're just like Mom. You never let me do anything!"

I stared at the empty stairs and sighed.

Maybe the soap had been mislabeled.

CHAPTER TWO

By the time I came downstairs to grab the Jeep keys, Ayla was nowhere to be found. I felt a pang of regret followed quickly by a spasm of relief—that rolled straight into a twinge of guilt. I didn't want to have another confrontation with her, but I also didn't want to leave the house without checking on her.

She might have run to Mom...well, no. She wouldn't have done that. At least, she wouldn't have sought out my mother to complain that I didn't involve her in cases. My mother was adamant that Ayla was too young to utilize her death speaker ability.

Which, if I was honest, was probably at least a part of my sister's frustration.

It likely wasn't all about me.

A quick trip around the house didn't turn her up, so I grabbed my keys and drove to the police department hoping to distract myself from the fight with an interesting case. However, I did make a mental note to get some alone time with my youngest sister when I returned from work that evening. Maybe take her to Griselda's for ice cream.

I hadn't been at the station for more than a few seconds when a sharp voice brought me out of my head in a hurry.

"Are you ever going to stop wearing that stupid outfit?" Jared Upton, the cantankerous old forensic investigator, asked me as soon as I slammed the Jeep door closed. He eyed me with cold attention. "You look ridiculous. Back in my day—"

"Jared, you're sixty-two years old, not ninety. You're too young to be lecturing people about your day. You still work here. This is *still* your day." I stopped respectfully as Jared pitched a cigarette butt into the gutter. "The captain doesn't have an issue with my outfit."

"It's distracting," he barked, his eyes drifting down toward my chest. He frowned at his own thoughts. "That just isn't appropriate."

I raised my eyebrow. "You know, they'd be there whether I was in this outfit or another one."

He took out a large white handkerchief and mopped his brow with it. "Hogwash. You girls know exactly what you look like in an outfit like that, and you do it on purpose. Besides, you're not a soldier anymore. So you shouldn't be dressed like one."

I smiled faintly, but quiet alarm bells were going off in my head.

Sure, this was my military outfit, and I continued to wear it because the magical defense woven into the very fabric was protection I could never replicate. The military had a department of magical tailors with varied skills, and all of those skills were used to create this outfit. Something like this might never be made again.

And yes, okay, the sleek bodysuit was formfitting—but it was also comfortable. It was the uniform I'd worn for eleven years. Every single day.

Regular clothes felt odd now.

But how did Jared Upton know *this* was a military outfit?

Sure, it was a standard-issue uniform in the ministry's military. Still, that military was made up of paranormal soldiers. Paranormopolis, the capital city of the supernatural world, was still unknown to humans.

Well, for the most part.

"I'm sorry, Jared, I'm confused. What did you mean by military outfit?" I asked.

Jared crumpled the handkerchief into a ball and stuffed it in his pocket. "I'm not here to answer questions for you," he snapped and then loudly explained his personal dislike of using psychics for police work. On and on and on he went, in a soliloquy of personal grievance and deep-seated resentment.

If there had been any other forensic investigator on the entire police force, I probably would've walked away. Since there wasn't?

I listened to his wordy dudgeon patiently.

You never know when you're gonna need a forensic investigator's help.

Especially in a police department.

"But if you were a real psychic, you would have known all that," he said finally, puffing up his chest in indignation. "And now you know how I really feel."

I'd been quiet long enough. "Well, we'll have to agree to disagree. I have no time to argue any of your points with you today, but thank you for sharing your in-depth perspective of personal pique with me. It's certainly something I will give all the attention it deserves." Which was none. "I hope you have a great day, Upton."

"You just stay out of my way, girly," Jared said harshly while dramatically stepping into my personal space.

Really.

I wanted to roll my eyes and walk away, but that would've been taking his bait. I would not give this craggy old man—the judgment based on action and not age—the satisfaction of knowing he was getting under my skin. "What do you have to say about that? Huh?"

"Stay out of your way?" I asked, keeping my voice level and professional. "I always stay out of your way, Jared. The only time I'm ever in your way is when you step in front of me to complain." I pointed. "Like now."

"Yeah, well, I have a lot of complaints about a lot of things," he said, crossing his arms over his chest and glowering.

He was so close his elbows brushed my chest, and I fought the urge to punch him in the nose. Instead, I just nodded and said, "I've noticed. You know, if you just gave the sexist, racist, ableist, ageist, misogynistic stuff a rest—"

"I'm not racist! How dare you say I'm racist! I

didn't say anything about anybody's race!" He threw his hands in the air. "Don't you dare say I'm racist!"

Did anyone else notice he didn't argue about any of the other *-ists* I named?

As soon as he raised his voice, the air around me became almost unbearably toxic, and I had to move back to get his rancid cigarette breath out of my face.

"Trying to find a victim, Upton?" a familiar voice asked.

I turned to see Cassie Blackwood, the police department's sixty-six-year-old receptionist, arriving on the scene. "Because if you are, I would say you're barking up the wrong tree. Astra doesn't take guff from anybody. I would also say that goes double for an opinionated old fart like you."

The man paled at the sight of her. "Too many damn women in this police department," Upton grumbled, and then hurried like his pants were on fire toward his car, keys in hand. "I'm taking my morning break, my lunch break, and my afternoon break over at the Hex Master. If you need me?" He glared. "Send a man to get me."

The Hex Master was the local dive bar. In Florida, alcohol couldn't be sold between midnight and seven a.m. in general. However, some localities had different rules in slightly different hours—for example, Miami-Dade county permits alcohol sales 24 hours a day, seven days a week. Because it's Miami.

Forkbridge, though, didn't try to make more work for itself if it didn't need to. So whatever the state rules were was just fine by our little town.

Anyway. The Hex Master opens every day just after sunrise.

Because alcoholics.

"What have you done to these men to make them all scared of you?" I asked the gray-haired woman as she came to stand next to me.

"Nothing they don't deserve," Cassie responded.

We watched Jared Upton race the engine of his restored 1976 AMC Pacer and back into traffic with a tire squeal. Mrs. Blackwood was a portly, cheerful-looking gray-haired old lady with kind eyes and a sharp tongue. At first glance, you wouldn't think she could make men run in fear.

But she could.

I chuckled. "No, seriously, I'm curious. You've never been anything but nice to me, and I find it hard to believe that a nice woman like you inspires the reaction that you do. But I see it with my own eyes. They're a little scared of you."

"I imagine so. Well, you know I grew up in Cassandra," she said as we walked toward the front door.

I nodded.

"When you're the daughter of a spiritualist, you get some invisible friends that hang out all your life. It's just a blip in their eternity, but it means you get a loyal lifelong friend. Those invisible friends? They're around all the time, so they take notice of bullies, I'll tell you." She winked. "Before I get too long-winded, let's just say a lot of the mean people that come through those doors find themselves with a poltergeist or two. And if they're mean to me? They definitely get two. At least." She shrugged. "Word gets around."

"Remind me not to get on your bad side, Mrs. Blackwood," I said, holding the door open for her. "The last thing I need is poltergeists."

THE LITTLE TOWN of Cassandra was the hot topic of conversation in the station, and not because of the big Halloween festival coming up at the end of the week.

"Well, they don't have a police force as such, so I don't see how they had any other choice," Officer Dietz told two younger officers as the three sipped paper cups of bad precinct coffee. "I'm surprised you two haven't heard about Cassandra."

"I mean, I know about it, but I ain't ever been there," the dark-haired officer responded. "Why would anybody go there? They ain't got nothing but that once-a-year Halloween party, and I heard that party gets weird."

"You know they didn't start out as a town, but Florida made them turn into one?" Dietz said with a harsh laugh. "They got a mayor forced on 'em, and that joke of a city council, but they still run things based on their hoodoo voodoo beliefs. No self-respecting normal person would move into that place and be subject to their crazy rules."

I'd almost made it past them, but stopped and stepped into their little circle at hearing the inaccurate drivel coming out of Dietz's mouth. "Hoodoo and Voodoo are not the same things," I told him. " The people that live in Cassandra are spiritualists. They don't practice Hoodoo or Voodoo."

"Nobody cares what they call it, Arden," Dietz snapped.

"Well, obviously you do. You're the one that brought it up."

"Of course you would say that. Neither do they believe in God," the young blond officer stated as he side-eyed me suspiciously. "Officer Dietz was being polite. My mama told me that they were devil worshipers. Terrible people. Never been in that town, never going to it."

"That's not true at all," I told him. "You're ridiculous. They're just people like anyone else. They get married, they have families, they send their kids to school. As far as religion, they absolutely do believe in a higher power beyond us, and they believe in spirit guides. They talk to spirits—"

"Any kind of spirits just scares me," the dark-haired one told the blond as if I hadn't been speaking. He then cast his eyes over me as if he just remembered who I was. "Besides, any woman who has that power in her could get away with anything! Especially that Gaea thing they talk about all the time."

For someone who would never go to the town of Cassandra, this guy sure seemed to know what they talk about. All the time, even.

I shook my head.

It was no wonder Emma couldn't find a decent partner in the station before I showed up. I wasn't used to people speaking so openly about their intolerance in front of me, but something seemed to have loosened the tongues of the Forkbridge PD today. Everyone was letting their opinions fly without a second thought.

Oh, right.

I almost forgot.

Halloween was this weekend.

The bigotry against paranormal-leaning folk in this part of Florida seemed to reach a fever pitch around Halloween. Despite Frick and Frack over here, everyone went to Cassandra. The only question was whether they went to celebrate or to protest.

I groaned inwardly.

The next week should be all kinds of fun.

"Well, that's one of the reasons Florida told them they had to have a regular town council," Dietz said. "Them hoodoo women couldn't keep their nose out of the affairs of regular folk."

"That's not what happened at all. And again, they don't practice Hoodoo," I told Dietz, but the three men ignored me as if I wasn't even there.

"Cassandra just eats up all the tourists, too,"

the blond cop chimed in as if he wanted to get every possible negative view of the Cassandran citizens into this one conversation. "Especially at Halloween. We'd have so much money for the police department if we could compete with them. But that town? That town sold its soul to the devil. They cause so many problems."

"Who does? The tourists?" I asked.

"No, the devil worshipers," he responded with an irritated nod. "I can't understand why they're even allowed to set up a town. They mock our way of life."

"What, by existing?" I asked incredulously.

Dietz glared at me and answered for the younger man. "Yes," he said, and then turned back to the other cops. "Look, you boys be on your guard. I've got a bad feeling about this week."

I crossed my arms. "Let me guess, you have this bad feeling every year?"

Dietz just gave me another look of barely hidden contempt.

It felt pointless to speak out against these views any more than I had. It wasn't worth the effort to reason with people that had made up their mind. They had no interest in hearing what anyone had to say that might challenge their worldview.

"You gentlemen have a good day," I told them and then turned on my heel.

"Wow. You look like you're in a rotten mood." Emma gestured toward the three men. "What was that about?"

I related the conversation to Emma.

"It sounds like they still look down on the spiritualists, which, to be fair, isn't exactly a surprise," she said. "Well, it's not fair, but you know what I mean. The preachers in Forkbridge get freaked out every Halloween like clockwork and stir up the locals. Every year, nothing happens in Cassandra other than a protest and a party—but Dietz might be right about this year being different."

"What do you mean?" I asked.

She glanced around and then leaned forward. "Last night, someone burned down the mayor's house. Like, smoldering ruin level burned down. So the house is basically a big pile of ashes."

I frowned and leaned closer. "The mayor of Forkbridge?"

"No. The mayor of Cassandra."

I sat down in the chair across from Emma.

"Oh. Yeah, I heard. Saw the news this morning. Weird, right?" A house in Cassandra being set on fire and then burning to the ground was out of character for the town, but something in Emma's expression told me there might be more to the story. I raised my eyebrow. "Was everyone okay? Was it arson or something?"

Now that I really thought about it, it was strange. The fire, I mean. The town was filled with spiritualists, which meant the place was filled to the brim with ghosts and spirits. Cassandra didn't need a comprehensive police force or fire department because the spirits that lived in the town saw everything and could sound an alarm within seconds of any crime or accident.

That they hadn't was...concerning.

"That's one of your more reasonable questions. Well, two reasonable questions," Emma said dryly. "Yes, the mayor got out of the house in time, and she's fine. Well, as fine as you can be after your house burns to the ground."

"Well, that's something, at least."

"And yeah, probably arson. I mean, the answer is probably yes, right?"

"I guess it will take a while for the investigation."

"Investigation. Right. Funny you should

mention that. Their fire department is all volunteer and doesn't have an investigative team, so no one can say for sure now whether it's arson. If left to their own devices they probably won't ever be able to decide. They just don't have the resources."

"Can't the state help?" I asked.

Emma gave me a look. "Do you remember who our governor is?"

"Right, sorry. So there's no information about this fire at all, other than it took place?"

"The only thing we know is the mayor said she saw a dark shape by her window, and something inside the house started to burn."

That still didn't sound right. The mayor had to have ghosts in and around her. They would know what happened and who, if anyone, did what. The spirits would've shared that information immediately.

My chair creaked as I shifted in it. "How do you know all this?"

Emma tapped a folder in front of her. "Captain Harmon told me as soon as I came in."

I gave a halfhearted nod toward the folder. "He started a file?"

"And then gave it to me—which is, natch, why it's sitting on my desk."

I blinked. "Wait. What do you mean he gave it to you?"

"Apparently, Cassandra has asked for help from their older sister city, and the mayor specifically requested the two of us. You can probably guess the reasons why. In any case, the captain agreed, and we've been assigned to help them out."

I looked at my phone. "You realize it's not even ten o'clock in the morning. What time did this fire happen?"

"About three in the morning." Emma glanced at her phone. "So, about six hours ago. Give or take."

"That moved fast." Almost...inhumanly fast.

See what I did there?

Emma shot me a glance. "What, you think the mayor should have waited three or four days to tell anyone? Anyway, they want us because they figure you'll be able to talk to spirits like you did with that actress case."

Ghosts were such gossips.

On Halloween, spirits were generally more active, but they should be even more active after a thwarted...whatever you wanted to call it. Arson? Attempted murder? Anyway, after an emotional disruption had a chance to settle in and fester, ghosts would travel toward it like sharks swarming chum in the water.

They loved high drama and high emotion and would be a fantastic resource...

...if we could interview them.

Which...we couldn't.

"You remember that I borrowed that ability from Ayla, right?" I reminded Emma. "I can't talk to ghosts on my own. That's not a skill I have. My mom does, and Ayla does, but I am not a death speaker."

"So borrow the ability from Ayla again," the detective said with a shrug. "I'm sure she'd be happy to lend it to you for a few days."

CHAPTER THREE

I opened the front door of Arden House (our family's gigantic home with a new age store attached) to see my sister Ayla standing with her fists balled and her feet apart, glaring at my other sister Althea. "This was supposed to be a tanning thing, Thea! You made me look like a Cheeto!" Dressed in a long black cloak, Ayla's bright orange skin did, in fact, look very much Cheeto-colored. "You and your stupid potions! Get it off! Now!"

"Anything I can help with?" I called down the hall as Emma came in behind me.

"Oh, wonderful. Now my failure will be witnessed by even more people," Althea muttered while squinting at Ayla. "It's always pleasant to have an audience observe a brightly colored mistake." Then, suddenly, she snapped her fingers and turned to survey an array of glass bottles. "Now, you can witness triumph. I think I know what might counteract that."

"You think you know? You think. Great. What are you complaining about, anyway?" Ayla whined angrily. "You're not the one that looks like a Cheeto, are you?" Upon spotting Emma, the youngest Arden sister made a harrumphing noise. "What are you two doing here? Aren't you supposed to be off fighting crime and making the city safe for Halloween?"

"You know, if Althea can't get that orange off your skin and you pair it with the right outfit? You might just be able to win the Halloween costume contest in Cassandra this weekend," Emma told my younger sister cheerfully.

"Right. Like anyone ever lets me out of this house," she told the detective disparagingly. "Everyone else can go wherever they want—"

"I can't," Althea mentioned without looking up from her bottles of ingredients. "Astra and Ami are over eighteen, Ayla. And Astra is, like, way over eighteen—"

"Watch it," I warned her. Thirty-three wasn't that old.

"As I was saying before our old maid sister got touchy, you and I are under eighteen, and neither one of us can drive." Althea glanced up. "Obviously, we're not going to have the same freedom as they are. It's nothing personal."

"You got to go on a case! You even fought pixies!"

"You got to go on a case, too, I seem to recall," Althea responded in a polite tone. "Granted, you weren't invited, you broke the rules to go, and I think Astra wanted to throttle you when she found you, but you did go on a case."

"Quit trying to make me not mad," Ayla shouted at Althea. She crossed her arms. "Work harder on making me not orange!"

Emma turned to look at me with a smile. "You know, I always wanted sisters."

"Did you?"

She nodded. "I did." She glanced over at Ayla and Althea. "Not so much anymore."

Ayla snorted, her orange nose wrinkling. "Right, because your vampire brother is such a prince."

"Hey," I said sharply, ready to criticize her rudeness—and then I forced myself to take a deep breath. I needed her cooperation, and jumping on her would not get it. "There's no reason to toss your bad mood on everyone. Look, we actually do need you for a case. We have a situation that probably involves ghost witnesses, and we need to be able to talk to them."

Ayla raised her eyebrow. "Oh?" The thirteen-year-old paused and considered the most prudent way to answer me. "You mean you need someone that can talk to ghosts," she said at last, an edge to her voice.

Emma frowned, looking confused. "Isn't that what Astra said?"

No, that wasn't what I said, and Ayla was making it clear that the voluntary handing-over of her valuable death speaker ability would not happen without a fight.

Assuming there was a snowball's chance in Hades it would happen at all.

Ayla considered me carefully and then looked at Emma. Finally, she narrowed her eyes and pulled herself up to full height. "I want to make it clear—again—that I've been waiting for this. You've been telling me that I'm ready. That I'm finally ready to not be a kid anymore." Ayla pointed at my chest. "Unless you want to out yourself as a stupid liar and someone not to be trusted, this is happening."

This speech—and her not-messing-around

vibe—would have been a lot more effective if Ayla didn't look like a carrot with a head of saffron.

I tried to keep my expression even, but suspect my face twitched with annoyance. Ayla wasn't wrong, per se—she and I'd been having a series of late-night discussions about her place in the Arden family and what she wanted to do with the rest of her life. She was much like I was at her age—impatient for adventure and desperate to grow up and be one of the adults.

Honestly, I imagined it was worse for her than it had been for me. Little Ayla was the baby of a six-woman family. It was an unenviable position to be in for someone trying to step from childhood into adulthood. Especially when two of her sisters were adults and the one closest to Ayla in age—Althea—acted like she had twenty years on her younger sister instead of just two.

Anyway, I told her she was ready to act more like an adult and leave childish things behind. That was true.

But her interpretation of my statement?

That wasn't precisely what I meant.

"Ayla, what I meant was that you were more than capable of acting like a grown-up. And that from my perspective, you were choosing, at times, to act like a child." I kept my voice down, and I didn't shout. "I just walked in here, and you were yelling at Althea. You've been nothing but snotty to Emma and me since we walked in. That's the type of stuff I've been encouraging you to leave behind."

"Right, because you're never snotty. Mom's never snotty. Aunt Gwennie—" Ayla stopped herself and looked uncomfortable. "Okay, Aunt Gwennie is never snotty, but she's a saint. I don't see why I have to drop my sass to have you respect me as an adult. None of the rest of you do."

Althea looked up. "But you're not an adult, Ayla. You're learning to be an adult. Sass shouldn't be barbed with resentment and anger and said with a desire to hurt, you know. If it is, it's not sass. It's just plain old cruelty." My fifteen-year-old sister appeared unbothered by Ayla's attitude or her Cheeto-like color. "You just need to learn not to take things so seriously or personally. That would solve half your problem right there."

Ayla shot Althea a dark look. "Right, says the witch that was born already seventy years old."

"Your fifteen-year-old sister is actually seventy years old?" Emma asked me, shocked. "I swear, every day, I learn something new about you people."

I shook my head. "Ayla's just insulting Althea's calm personality. If Ayla is the fire, Thea's the rocks around the fire ring that keep it contained. My sister is particularly levelheaded to an almost unnatural degree."

"I can't help it if I'm an old soul with sangfroid," Althea shrugged.

"So, as entertaining as this is," the detective responded with an eye roll, "we need to get going and start this investigation." Emma looked at Ayla. "I know you've had your fun with your foot-stomping temper tantrum, but Astra wasn't kidding. We've been asked to investigate arson that might have been witnessed by ghosts. We need you to let your sister borrow your ability again."

"No, you don't. You just need to bring me along."

"As much as I appreciate your enthusiasm for law enforcement, Ayla, I don't know anything about what we're walking into. It's not even an area I normally work in, so we're going to be on our own," Emma pointed out. "If we get into trouble, I can't just call the police cruiser to show up and back me up. They can't cross the town line."

"But I know how to call a bunch of ghosts to get us help. Astra doesn't."

"Why don't you just bring Mom?" Althea asked, infuriating Ayla.

I shook my head. "Because the investigation is in Cassandra."

"What investigation is in Cassandra?" my mother asked, alarmed, as she entered the room.

WE EXPLAINED the situation to my mother.

"Impossible," she insisted with a very definite firmness. "The Cassandra spiritualists have a population of at least two hundred and fifty ghosts in that town at any one given time. Most of the time, there are more ghosts than there are people. No local would commit a crime in Cassandra because they would know—" My mother stopped talking and looked oddly at Emma and then at me.

"They would know who committed the crime almost immediately because a ghost would see and immediately tell someone. I already explained that to Emma, but that didn't happen in this case." I opened the case folder, scanned it, and handed the right notes to my mother. She read it, frowning. "The captain said they asked for us because they don't know who did it or even how it happened. They need outside help."

"Ayla, have you spoken to anyone undead this morning that could give us insight into what's happening?" my mother asked my bright orange sister. She then turned and leaned toward Althea. "Go finish correcting your sister's color, please. She looks like an orange from one of the orchards."

"Orange!" Althea shouted, glancing up from her bottles. "Mom, you're a genius."

"Yes, dear." My mother turned back toward Ayla. "Ayla?"

"I haven't seen any ghosts this morning," she said. Ayla then lowered her voice and looked around the table. "Or...maybe I have." She wasn't old or experienced enough to hide the sly little grin.

"Pardon me?" my mother asked sharply.

"What! You know you can't go to Cassandra because you're the high priestess," Ayla told my mother. "That's the one agreement we had with them, that there was a line the two leaders wouldn't cross. Right? You made me read that stupid agreement before I was ten."

My mother didn't blink, and her stare only tightened as Ayla's tone challenged her self-control.

"Well, I'm not a high priestess, and I may just be a young priestess and stuff, but I can go into Cassandra. I know that much. I can cross the boundary. I can help Emma and Astra with this case. So, I'm probably meant to, or something." She looked down at her hands. "Well, once I'm not orange anymore." Ayla looked up at my mother, a pleading look on her face. "I could stomp my foot, and I could complain that you never let me go anywhere, and you never let me use my powers, but that's not even why."

"It isn't, is it?" Mom asked her with an unsparing stare.

Ayla looked suddenly nervous.

"You have the floor, Priestess," my mother told her in the stern high priestess voice that warned anyone on the other end of it to watch their next step. "Explain to us why, despite your behavior, we should trust you to represent this family coven in this manner."

Oh boy.

"You know," she began nervously, her fingers

twisting the buttons on her cloak, "like I said, I can cross the boundary. That's just one reason—"

"So can Astra, if you give her your ability," my mother responded. "That's not an argument that tells us why you should be the one to do this and no other."

"And that's the other reason. I can give Astra my power. But I can't give her my ability," my youngest sister argued, her nervousness melting away. She blinked hard, moved forward, and poked her index finger on the table. "I can't give Astra my relationships, the knowledge of the different ghosts that I've built up over the years. Since I was little. Althea can't transfer the gossip I've heard about Cassandra with a potion—"

Althea lifted her head. "If you give me—"

"Hush," my mother told her, and she hushed.

Ayla nodded excitedly. "What about my knowledge of the different spiritualists' relationships?" She looked around the table. "I know more about Cassandra than anyone here because I talk to them all the time. I've been talking to the ghosts that have been hanging out in that town for years. They're my friends."

The detective was the first to speak.

"She's got a point," Emma said reluctantly. "I'm not overly enthusiastic about taking any thirteen-year-old on an investigation—even one I suspect is a big pile of nothing. But I've been doing a lot of things I never thought I would do. Oddly enough," she added cheerfully, "it's been working out."

"Considering Ayla's attitude lately, I don't know that you can trust her," my mother told Emma as Ayla's face fell. "All of the things she said? Those things are absolutely true. Her arguments are well thought out, and I agree with them. And if she were better behaved or more mature?" My mother raised her palms up as if silently presenting a chest of Ayla's recent maturity missteps to her.

The girl's eyes dropped, and her cheeks flushed pink.

"But she hasn't been acting very mature lately, and that chip she's got on her shoulder might get in the way of listening to your directions"—my mother stared intently at Ayla—"because it seems to be blocking her ears of late."

"I just want a chance," she whispered, her downcast eyes filling with tears.

"Ayla Arden, you are a priestess of the great goddess Athena," my mother told Ayla harshly. "This is a council of the coven to discuss what is to be done for people that need our help. This"—

my mother slammed her palm down on the table with a slap—"is not about you. It's not about what you want. You don't seem to realize it's those tears in your eyes for your own situation, your own wants and desires and needs, that cause me to have concerns." Ayla's delicate flush turned fiery hot. "Your focus should not be on yourself right now, but on the others you seek to serve."

I felt terrible for my sister and interfered against my better judgment. "Mom, come on. You don't think that's a little harsh?" I asked.

She shot me a look. "Did you ever cry to a superior officer because you didn't get the assignment you wanted? Did you ever stomp your foot and yell at your superiors because they made decisions you were unhappy with? Did you allow your soldiers more concern for themselves than those you served and served for?"

Reluctantly, I shook my head no.

"No one gets to demand adult respect while acting like a child," my mother said as she turned her gaze back to Ayla.

"But Mom, she is a kid," Althea, also a kid, pointed out.

"But she doesn't want to be. I didn't tell her to grow up too fast," my mother told Althea. "This treatment is by her request and her own design."

Before I could add something else to the discussion, Ayla stood up.

My mother stared across at her. "Well?"

She took a deep breath. "You're right. I'm sorry. My attitude has been immature and resentful, and I shouldn't be acting like that. But, I can do this." Ayla moved around the table, head high, to stand next to my mother. "May I make a request of my high priestess?"

My mother looked at her with suspicion...but finally nodded.

In one motion, Ayla dropped to her knee and stared up into my mother's surprised face. "High priestess, I respectfully request your permission to assist Astra and Emma on their case. I oath to listen to their directives and selflessly focus only on our goals of service to those in need. I will act responsibly in honor of the goddess Athena." She bowed her head. "I will only do this with your permission and your leave."

The surprised expression on my mother's face wouldn't have been more pronounced if Ayla had launched herself across the table and punched my mother in the nose. Mom looked at Aunt Gwennie—who, as always, had been watching silently from the side—and the two seemed to share a silent communication over the bowed head of my thirteen-year-old sister.

Mom turned toward Emma and me. "You will ensure that she is safe, and if you cannot do that as your first priority, you will bring her back to this house." Her eyes narrowed. "Without delay."

It wasn't a question.

"We will," I assured my mother.

"You may serve, Ayla of the Arden coven," my mother said finally in her deep, resonating high priestess voice. "But you have oathed to us here in the covenstead with your request, and I will hold you to those oaths as if you gave them to the goddess herself." Mom reached down and tilted Ayla's still-bowed head up. "And if you continue to foot stomp and throw temper tantrums like a child, making their work more difficult for them?"

"Yes?"

"I will ground you until you're twenty-one. Are we clear?"

"Yes." Ayla bobbed her head up and down.

My mother frowned. "Yes, what?"

"Yes, ma'am," she repeated, standing up to her full height.

"Fine. Then go get ready for your first act of service," Mom told her. "And get ready to earn that adult respect you want so desperately. A chance has been given. It's up to you to take it and make the most of it."

EMMA PULLED me aside as we waited for Ayla to get changed.

"What was all that about? A contract between you guys and Cassandra?"

I explained a little bit about spiritualists and witches and how the spiritualists believed themselves to be non-occult, non-magic, non-paranormal. "To them, it's just a religious thing, and they don't like witches all that much. They think we're the evil opposite of them or something."

"And your mother is banned from the town?" Emma asked, her eyebrow raised.

"Not my mother specifically. Whoever the high priestess is. They don't have a particular issue with my mother."

Emma thought about it for a minute. "Hold on. They asked for us. No, not just us. You. The captain mentioned they wanted you specifically." Her face twisted. "Don't they know you're an Arden and a member of the coven?"

"I'm not, though," I told Emma. "You take oaths as an adult. I never did."

"She is still a member as the daughter of a high priestess," Aunt Gwennie told Emma as she joined us. "Just not an inner circle member. But what you're thinking is correct, Emma. Under normal circumstances, they would not welcome Astra into their town. They certainly wouldn't want to ask for her help."

"I feel like I just walked into one of the *Twilight* movies. Anyway. Then why did they?" Emma asked, her expression concerned.

That was a good question.

CHAPTER FOUR

*L*illian Thornton lives—or rather, lived—down a dirt road in a tall, angular house with a sprawling lawn that leads to a gleaming lake.

Witch Lake.

The small body of water buttressed up against the spiritualist encampment that became the town of Cassandra was rumored to have been the site of local witch trials hundreds of years ago. The more far-fetched rumors used those waters to explain the well-known phenomenon of the town's mediums and "spirit guides."

I glanced at the water and frowned.

Trials.

More like state-sanctioned torture and murder.

Historical trials are not always as you imagine them to be—a judge, a jury, evidence. Witnesses. Sure, some witch trials probably looked just like that. People gathered in a courtroom to judge whether someone was or wasn't guilty of some crime, a rational examination of facts.

But they also had trials by ordeal.

The prayer test involved making an accused witch read bible passages as it was believed we witches were incapable of doing so. Do you know who else was incapable of doing so?

Illiterate people.

And yet recitation of the passage was no guarantee of innocence, if the town wanted you dead. George Burroughs, in Salem? Flawlessly recited the Lord's Prayer from the gallows just before his execution. Did they cut him down, stop his execution?

Nope. It was dismissed as just another satanic trick.

There was also the ordeal by water.

Accused witches were dragged by townsfolk to the nearest body of water, where they were stripped to their skivvies, bound, and then tossed in to see if they would sink or float.

If you float?

You're a witch.

If you sink, you're innocent of the accusation.

While most people like to point out innocence isn't all that valuable to a drowned suspect once dead, victims typically had a rope tied around their waists to hoist them up once they were underwater for enough time to prove themselves. But sufficient time and proof can be subjective, and accidental drowning deaths were not unheard of.

"This property is stunning," Emma said as the three of us stepped out of her Chevy Malibu. She took a look around and noted two neighboring houses an acre apart in either direction. "This is clearly not cheap. That smoldering heap of ash is also on a hill. Those neighbors would have seen it the moment it went up."

"No streetlights," I pointed down the dirt road toward the paved street. "If someone drove up here to set it on fire, not sure the neighbors would have been able to see anything."

There was no one nearby. The smoking heaps of ash had gone oddly unnoticed until we pulled up, and there was nothing left of the house that had once stood two stories tall.

"Ayla, is there anyone here?" I asked my

younger sister as she squinted in the sun. "Do you see any ghosts hanging around?"

She glanced around the property with a good deal of disappointment written clear across her face. "I don't see anyone hanging around. There are no ghosts anywhere. Like, the whole place is just empty." The longer Ayla looked around, the more her expression morphed from disappointment to concern. "Astra, this isn't normal. I mean, there are tons of ghosts in Cassandra, right?"

"So we've been told."

"And ghosts—in general—rush to the site of emotional drama. So there should be at least a few here. The fact that there's not is weird."

"Well, the mayor isn't here, and none of the investigators are here, so maybe the ghosts went to wherever those people are," Emma guessed. She pulled out her tablet and squatted down, trying to block the bright sunlight from the screen. With a few taps, the detective nodded and looked up.

"Apparently, they're all in town in the meeting hall. It also conveniently serves as a police station, so I say we head over there."

"They don't have a police station?" Ayla asked Emma.

"I thought you talk to the ghosts that come in and out of here all the time?" the detective responded suspiciously. "I would've guessed you knew more about the town than me."

"I wasn't talking to the ghosts to get information to do a book report for school on Cassandra. For one, I'm homeschooled, and my mother is the teacher, so it's not like she would want me to do a report on this place with independent information. And second, I never told my mother I was talking to ghosts until recently, so I was pretty careful about what I asked." Ayla's words ran together as she anxiously defended her knowledge of this strange little Florida town. "When I see a ghost I know, I'll be able to ask. So don't you worry about that."

Emma put her tablet away. "I'm not really worried about whether you can talk to ghosts at the moment. I'm worried about the fact that that's a suspected crime scene, and there's nobody here to guard it. Which, to be frank, makes me wonder if someone's pulling our leg here." She leaned against her Malibu and surveyed the area. "No one's bothered to come here and ask us what we're doing on this property, either."

"Well, the ghosts would probably tell them, you know," Ayla pointed out.

Emma raised her eyebrow. "You just said you don't see any ghosts here."

"Just because I don't see them here doesn't mean they're not here."

Emma cast a sidelong glance at Ayla. "What does that mean? You can see the ghosts, or you can't see the ghosts? I thought the whole reason we brought you on this little field trip was so you could talk to the ghosts, Trixie Belden." I fought back a snort at the reference to the thirteen-year-old fictional detective. "If you can't see them, how can you talk to them?"

Ayla crossed her arms and sighed with a weariness that weighed down her voice. "Yes, Detective, to talk to them, I have to see them, that's true. But that doesn't mean they have to be seen all the time." Ayla looked up, scanning the clouds as if searching for a simple explanation Emma would understand. "Ghosts aren't like us. They're not anchored to bodies, right? They're just spirit, and spirit can go wherever it wants."

"If you say so. But I understand what you're saying," Emma said with a nod.

"Spirit can also look any way it wants, you know? Like, it can be a tree or a dog or horse or a bird or a lake. Spirit can be anything. Ghosts are spirits that are really attached to the life they left behind, and they decide to be who they were when they were human because they don't want to be anything else. Or they don't know how to be anything else. So that could happen, too."

"Still following you," Emma told her.

"But death doesn't change that they're ghosts, and they're spirit even if they choose to keep looking like themselves. So they can pop in and out of appearing like their human forms or whatever forms they have chosen. They can also be invisible. Spirit doesn't have to be seen."

"You and the priest at my church would get along really well. He confuses me half the time, too," Emma said and then glanced around. "Okay, so you're saying they could be here watching us. They could be listening to everything we're saying, and we would never see them? We would never know they were here. You included."

"Yeah, that's what I was getting at. I just want you to understand—"

"Okay, Trixie, let me explain something to you about me. I'm a detective. I care about one thing. Solving the case. To solve the case, I care about many little things, but I don't need a lot of context for explanations. I just need the facts. You understand?"

Ayla nodded with a trace of nervousness.

I reached out to lay a comforting hand on her shoulder. "Ayla, it's okay. Just realize a lot of what Mom teaches you, all of this extra information?" I added. "It's just that. Extraneous. When we're investigating a case, we want to get the facts and the information together as quickly as possible. We try to accomplish what we need to accomplish and move on." Ayla nodded. "You know how Mom tells you to explain tears and flowers about the ins and outs of spiritual law to the humans?"

"Yeah, that's what I was doing, because—"

"Yeah, don't do that here." Emma turned around and gestured toward the doors on her Malibu. "If I need a deeper explanation about something, I'll ask you for it. I believe in ghosts, so I don't need you to prove it to me or anything. I just want to know what they saw. And I want to know if you can talk to them. And I want to know what role they might have played. Other than that?" Emma yanked the car door open with a loud creak. "Just stick to what you're here for. Be succinct, to the point, and you'll do fine."

"Center of town?" I asked as I climbed into the car.

"Yep." Emma looked over us to ensure we

were buckled up before she started the car. "Time to go swimming in crazy town!"

This should be entertaining.

THE HALL WAS ALMOST COMPLETELY PACKED with people. Small groups of men, women, and children huddled together, whispering to one another. Periodically, a head would poke out of a huddle here or there and cast a glance toward the front, only to vanish back into the huddle.

The room, which was crammed with people dressed in costumes that would have looked right at home at any Renaissance Faire, had a nervous stillness to it.

Apprehensive energy.

"The ghosts disappearing from the town likely has nothing to do with the mayor's house catching on fire last night," a young woman in a bright red sundress told the assembled citizens. "Besides, we all know that ghosts can choose to appear or not appear as is their will. Who are you to question their will, Bill Platt?"

A man in a greasy work shirt barked back, his voice booming across the large gathering place. "Don't you make this about religion or faith or whatever it is you're about to do, Serena Bliss," the man said. "That isn't the point of this conversation."

Some people made a show of facing away from the two while others smiled or nodded in agreement.

Serena Bliss, at the front of the room, crossed her arms. Behind her, a bright fire raged in the fireplace, casting flickering shadows on the wall. Despite the fact that it was fall in Florida, the room was icy.

Or maybe that was just everybody glaring at one another.

A man in an ornate red and black vest cut in. "Of course it's about faith, Bill. That's the only thing that matters. The spirits have been with us for generations."

"Let him speak," Serena told the vested man, who nodded. "Bill, what is it about for you, then?"

"It's about the fact that we've tasked these ghosts with guarding the town. Not to mention the fact that the only money we get comes from you, the readers, who interpret what the dead have to say to those who come here." He looked around the room at the worried expressions on everyone's faces. "I'm not sure about the rest of you, but I own a gas station. If the ghosts have vanished and we need to start paying for security, what should we do?" He snorted in disbelief. "I've warned you people about this, that we needed to start offering other services. If they don't come back, I might be one of the only people left with a job."

"Well, perhaps they left this town because of doubters like you," Serena Bliss responded with a toss of her waist-length straight blond hair. "We are only blessed with their presence because we work hard to deserve it. Perhaps we no longer deserve the bounty and boons that the spirits have given us all these years."

The three of us hung toward the back. We watched the townsfolk bicker with one another over the meaning of the ghosts' appearance and subsequent disappearance.

"Or maybe it was them witches over in Forkbridge that finally decided to make a move," the gruff Platt responded. A low buzz of whispers rose in agreement with the gas station owner. "Has anybody even checked with them to see if Satan's hags cursed us for some perceived offense?"

Emma turned and looked at my sister and me. "Satan's hags?"

"They don't like us very much," I told her with a shrug.

"And yet they don't even realize two of the hags are standing at the back of their meeting hall," the detective pointed out as she scanned the crowd. "No wonder they depend on the ghosts for information. These people don't have an observant bone in their bodies. I'd have to rate their tactical judgment an F."

"Where is the mayor?" someone called from the crowd.

"Yeah, you're not the mayor, Serena! We don't want to hear from you. We want to hear from the mayor," agreed another from the other side of the room.

"Who is that?" I whispered to Ayla.

"Serena Bliss?" she asked me. I nodded. "She's the daughter of Joy Bliss. She used to be the spiritual leader of this place. Joy, not Serena, I mean. Serena is like the right hand woman of the current spiritual leader."

"And who is that?" Emma whispered.

"Bernard Gerald. He took over when Joy Bliss died."

"Interesting. I wonder how that sat with Serena," I murmured.

Serena Bliss stood in front of the townsfolk

on an elevated platform. Her head was high, her posture was straight, and she had her hands clasped in front of her like a nun. Despite the apparent calm, her ice blue eyes twitched with irritation. "As I have told you previously, the mayor is already in seclusion with Guru Bernie to prepare for the Halloween festival."

"Guru Bernie?" the three of us whispered at once.

I looked at Emma. "Tell me that is not the most Florida thing you've ever heard. Guru Bernie." I snorted. "That's the most ridiculous name. And I've met pixies."

"Be nice," she admonished me. "Remember, you're here representing the Forkbridge Police Department, the Forkbridge community, and these people already think you're Satan's hag. So try not to give them any proof of that."

"My bad. I'll behave."

"She's the boss of you?" Ayla asked, her eyes wide.

"Yep," I told her without hesitation. "Regarding police stuff and human stuff? She sure is. She's the detective. I'm assisting her."

Ayla turned toward us. "So, wait. Are you the boss on paranormal stuff?"

I shrugged. "I guess. Never really thought about it."

Emma nodded. "Pretty much."

She scrunched up her face. "You can't both be the bosses."

"Sure we can. We each have different skills. I'm not gonna be in charge when the issue relates to something that Emma is an expert in. Obviously, she's not going to be in charge when I'm the expert in a situation. This is how we work together." I tilted my head and raised my eyebrow. "In all your homeschooling, you've never heard the concept of teamwork?"

"Well, yeah, as far as the coven. But Mom is always in charge, and we always follow. She says there has to be just one person as the leader. There can't be two."

"Of course she said that," I murmured.

"That's one person's opinion," Emma told her cheerfully. "Astra and I happen to have a different opinion. And we have a different way of working than your mom."

"So my mom's wrong?"

Emma became visibly unsettled. "Um. I didn't say that, and I would really appreciate it if you didn't relate to her that I said anything resembling that, either. But, anyway, Ayla, people choose to work together in a lot of different ways. Sometimes they work together as equals, and sometimes one person is in charge. Sometimes they tag off. It all just depends on the people involved."

We were so engrossed in our little leadership debate that none of us realized the entire meeting hall was filled with angry Cassandran citizens…

…staring at us.

"WHAT ARE YOU DOING HERE?" Serena Bliss inquired sharply across the room, standing on the dais above everyone else. "This is a private meeting for those that live here in Cassandra, and outsiders are not welcome."

"Forgive us appearing to intrude, ma'am," Emma called back without moving toward the front. It enabled her to shout across the entire meeting hall, ensuring that everyone in attendance could hear her. "My name is Detective Emma Sullivan from the Forkbridge Police Department. We've been asked to assist in the investigation of Mayor Lillian—"

"Asked to assist? Forkbridge people? You must be mistaken. Who asked you to come here?"

Serena asked acidly, cutting off Emma's introduction. "I am the right-hand of both the mayor and the guru, and I can assure everyone here I did not ask for any outside assistance."

"Because it's always about you, right, Serena?" an unidentified voice murmured just loud enough to be heard.

Emma cleared her throat. "As far as I understand it, ma'am, the mayor herself made the request of Captain Harmon," she responded loudly and respectfully. "We've only been here for a few minutes." Silence. "We went out to the property and saw no one, so we came looking for people to talk to so we could get started. Also, y'all listed this place as your makeshift police station."

"That witch is with her!" a woman shouted.

Someone else yelled, "Two witches! That's the girl that talks to the ghosts and corrupts them!" Ayla shrank closer to me.

"Why would you bring witches into our town? They are not—"

"If you're about to say we're not allowed here, I suggest you look at the treaty between the guru and the high priestess. Borders and boundaries only apply to the two of them," I told the crowd. "I'm not here to do anything other than help you all figure out who wanted to burn down your mayor's house—if anyone did—and to hopefully get this resolved before this weekend."

As people argued among themselves, there was a flurry of shouting.

"Shut up! All of you!" Serena yelled firmly. The room quieted. "If the mayor has sent for you, there must be a reason," Serena answered with a tight jaw. "If you'll make your way up here, I will bring you to see the mayor and the guru."

A man yelled from the other side of the room, his voice ringing through the hall. "You can't bring Satan's hag to see the guru!"

"If the mayor has called for these women, then it was with the guru's permission." The woman's face hardened. "If it was not with the guru's permission, then we should have a recall vote immediately to remove her as mayor. Perhaps the smoke has addled her mind and judgment."

"I think it's addled your mind and your judgment if you're gonna bring those witches into the same room with the guru!" screamed a heavy-featured woman with shoulder-length gray hair. "What if she tries to curse him!"

"My skill is psychometry," I explained to the terrified woman as I raised my gloved hands. "I'm not the high priestess, and I'm not going to put a

curse on anyone. My sister is a death speaker"—
who can translocate things, but let's not mention
that to these freaked out people right now—"and
can speak to the dead the same as you all. So you
have nothing to fear from us. You have my word."

The crowd, which had been growing
increasingly boisterous, began to quiet down.
"The word of a witch," someone muttered. "Like
that means anything."

As we neared the front of the room, a few
individuals attempted to obstruct our progress.
One in particular was a large man with a square
jaw who stood out from the crowd. I only noticed
him because he chose to give Ayla a menacing
look as we tried to pass him by.

Who tries to intimidate a thirteen-
year-old kid?

I felt the anger bubble up.

I took a step toward him, determined to
explain why big men shouldn't step up on
children, but an elderly woman with a scar
covering the left side of her face stepped forward
just as I did. She continued to glare at him until
he took a step back, turned around, and walked
away from us.

The elderly woman never said a word, but she

did give us a silent nod and a wave to indicate that we should follow her.

I looked back at Ayla. "It's okay."

My sister looked up at me and swallowed. "Yeah, I don't think you're right, Astra. Something's not right here. Something's not right at all."

CHAPTER FIVE

a s we left the meeting hall, Serena Bliss led us to a small cottage in the middle of an enclosed square. Archie, my familiar owl, was perched on the back of a patio chair, cleaning his feathers. He looked up at me and fluttered his wings, dropping a few sand grains as he did so.

"Nice to see you," I said to the previously absent owl. "Were you too busy this morning to wait around?"

"You know, the only reason I'm here is in case the star card flips over, and we have to rush to save someone that needs it. And by here, I mean here in this steamy heat trap of a state." Archie paused as he shook his tail feathers. "Now, don't get me wrong, Florida has its drawbacks, but it also has a lot of critters. Tasty critters, at that. I catch my breakfast, lazybones, so sometimes it takes a while." He tilted his head and glanced at Emma and Ayla. "What are you doing here?"

"The mayor of Cassandra asked us to come to investigate a fire at her house last night. Well, her former house, to be more precise." I gestured toward Serena, who had stopped her slow walk to stare at me suspiciously. "This rather dour woman is leading us to where the mayor and guru are holed up."

"So frustrating that I can't hear him," Emma sighed.

"He's not really saying much," Ayla told her. "You're not missing anything."

"I beg your pardon?" Serena snapped. "What are you all talking about?"

Just then, a window flew open, and new age music blared from the tiny bungalow. "I didn't tell you anything of the sort, you dirty old man!" an angry shout pierced through a barrage of drums and chimes. We all turned to stare at it. "What on earth happened to you? I swear, it's like you're someone else!"

Serena stared at Ayla and me with suspicion.

What the heck did she think we had to do with it?

The woman with the ironic name snapped, "I need to go intercede between guru and the mayor."

"Do you do that a lot?" I asked her.

She didn't answer.

As the four of us hurried around a walkway toward the front door, the noise of the argument continued to invade the wildflower-filled courtyard. As a woman's voice—which let loose a torrent of aggrieved complaints and frustrations into every silence—was responding, a man's voice laughed somewhat scornfully.

"You did say this is where your spiritual leader lives?" I asked Serena skeptically. "I got that right, didn't I? That's the guru?"

She came to a halt once more, pencil straight, her expression stern and above the cacophony of words bombarding our ears. "The guru is a great man," Serena volunteered without answering the question. "He exudes the charisma of a charismatic leader, but lately, he's teaching lessons in a different way and...it can be misunderstood." She turned away from us immediately and continued toward the front of the bungalow.

"I told you this was going to be fun. A crazy guru, a screeching mayor, and a mysterious assistant to them both, that just screams hidden agenda," Emma said with an eyebrow wiggle and then took off after the severe Serena Bliss. Ayla stared after the detective, a confused look on her face. "Come on, Trixie Belden, what are you waiting for?" she asked my sister without turning around.

"Why is she so happy?" Ayla asked me.

"No one's dead, and it's something different."

Among the items on the front porch were a large pot of pink flowers and another with what appeared to be herbs. There was also a small table and two chairs, as well as a wooden clothes hanger with a white sheet draped over it. From the top of the stairwell, a huge jack-o-lantern grinned at us.

The front door was thrown open with a thud as if by magic.

"You want me to sleep on the couch? I've got no problem with that. You want to sleep on the sidewalk under the stars and give me the bungalow? I'll be happy to go get some blankets. Do you want to sleep outside tonight? Fine. But you and I are not sleeping–" spotting us, the woman broke off her angry rant.

"Who are you people? Serena, what is the meaning of this?"

SHE WAS a petite woman in her late fifties or early sixties, with long gray hair pulled back in a tight ponytail, and a piercing blue gaze. She wore a salmon-colored sarong around her waist and a tied-on halter top that exposed her midriff.

The woman didn't look like any mayor I'd ever seen.

"Mayor Thornton?" Detective Emma Sullivan asked, as if she, too, couldn't quite believe the island-chic woman could be a mayor. "Are you Mayor Lillian Thornton?"

She stood on the porch and looked down at us. "Yes, that's right. You are?"

"My name is Emma Sullivan. I'm a detective with the Forkbridge Police Department. The captain, who I believe you're acquainted with, sent my partner and me over here to help you folks." Emma paused. "Concerning the fire last night?"

Hearing her words, the mayor appeared to go slightly limp with relief. "That dear man," Lillian Thornton said as she waved us in. "Thank you so much for coming. I can't tell you how grateful I am that you did. Come, come!"

As the door opened, Serena Bliss stepped

forward to ensure that she was the first person through. Mayor Thornton frowned and shifted her gaze from Emma to me, as if she were worried about how we would perceive her if she allowed this entitlement to go unanswered. After a split second or two, the mayor said nothing—at least until a ferocious dachshund barked at us as we approached the bungalow.

Lillian Thornton sighed, lifted the small, yapping dachshund from the floor, and wrapped it in her arms. "Okay, Hedy, calm down. These people are here to help us. I know you've had a rough night, but let's not bark at the police officers, okay?" Hedy gave her a few licks, one last bark, and then quieted down.

"Your dog is adorable," Ayla told the woman.

"Thank you. Despite her attempt to convince you otherwise, she's not nippy or aggressive, so you're welcome to pet her," the mayor said affably and jerked her chin toward the couch. "Have a seat. Can I get any of you anything to drink?"

Even after losing her home, the mayor was the picture of Southern hospitality.

Well, if Southern hospitality wore a salmon sarong.

Which, frankly?

It generally didn't.

"Were you unable to find a babysitter, Detective?" the mayor asked, glancing at Ayla.

"Hey! I'm here to help!" she blurted out, unable to hide her feeling of offense.

"Why don't we take a seat," I suggested, jumping in before Ayla could rev up, and sat down on the couch. The others followed—including the scowling Serena Bliss (who sat directly beside me).

Lillian Thornton took the chair opposite and leaned forward, her elbows on her knees, cradling the dog in her lap. She gave Serena a long look.

Serena stared back.

No one said anything, not even Hedy, as we watched the silent tension between the two women.

Finally, the blond woman turned a bright red and sat up ramrod straight, crossing her arms. "I am your assistant and his. I need to be here. So just stop it."

Lillian smiled serenely but didn't answer—and didn't agree.

From the couch, I had a reasonable view of the rest of the bungalow and the surrounding area. The sunlight was blocked out by dark blue drapes in the living room. Despite this, the lamps and candles allowed me to clearly see the portrait of Guru Bernie meditating, on the wall above the fireplace. There were also various scenes of people dressed in white robes and flanked by palm trees, which were particularly striking.

Many included the mayor, smiling and happy.

I noticed very few included Serena Bliss.

Suddenly, a male voice rasped, "What a silly gathering, for a silly reason."

The old man was sitting cross-legged on the kitchen floor, dressed in a turban and blue sweatpants, with a smirk on his face. He giggled, his hand resting against his bare chest, as if he were a schoolgirl.

Lillian Thornton flinched. "Bernard, please—"

"Like my new headgear?" he asked Serena, ignoring the mayor and pointed to the turban perched atop his head.

"Yes, Guru."

He unwrapped it and threw the heavy fabric with a pattern of stars onto the floor in front of her. "It matches my drapes a little. With stars," the old man added. "Cosmic, right? Doesn't it make you think of the cosmos?"

"Yes, Guru," she answered.

With a jerky movement, Guru Bernie's expression changed from childlike to menacing.

He raised his eyebrows and tilted his head to the side. "Why don't you all just meditate on the fire? I mean, that's what we all claim we believe in, right?" He reached down, grabbed a pack of cigarettes, and lit one.

I stared, shocked and disbelieving.

Something wasn't right here.

The Cassandran citizens were well known to be anti-smoking, anti-drinking—anti- anything not hippie-dippy natural, if you want to know the truth.

Taking a deep drag on his cigarette, the guru blew a ring of smoke toward Emma. "You could do with some meditation, you uptight—"

"Bernard!" Thornton shouted sharply.

Emma and I exchanged a glance, and I could tell exactly what she was thinking. That's because it was exactly what I was thinking at the time. What kind of spiritual guru, exactly, was this individual? This was the leader of the town with the highest mediumship per capita on the planet? The gateway to the spirit world?

I mean, seriously?

Turning back to us, the mayor smiled wearily and scratched Hedy between the ears. "As you can imagine, we're so...flustered right now. And there's so little I can tell you. I'd gone out to eat

with Bill when I got the call, rushed home, and–"
She swallowed as if overcome by emotion. "We
would very much like to know how this
happened. I have insurance, so I'm not too
concerned about that. But with it being so close
to Halloween? I'm afraid it could be a hate crime."

"A hate crime?" I asked. "Why would you
think that?"

"The rituals this weekend must take place,"
Serena explained, answering my question. "If this
is the first attack of many, or if this was done to
stop the Halloween celebration, we have to find
the perpetrator and ensure the festivities take
place." She glanced at the guru. "It's imperative."

"You seem very sure someone did this on
purpose," I observed.

"Well. I mean if someone did." Serena stared
back at me. "Which we don't know. Of course. That
appears to be why you people are here. To find out."

Uh huh.

Emma pulled out her notepad. "So you
weren't in the house when it happened?" Mayor
Thornton shook her head no. "Did you see
anything unusual last night when you left for
dinner? Anyone close to the house? Any threats
that you might have received?"

"I'm sorry, Detective, you know as much as I do. The fire department said there was, ah, some type of accelerant used." She wrapped her arm around Hedy, her expression stressed. "So the fire spread quickly. There's a fire man–"

A fire department? Then why did we get called?

"A fireman," Guru Bernie corrected her pronunciation to make it sound more like one word instead of two. His voice was back to his amused, childlike lilt, and he was no longer smoking. "Just because they meditate on fire doesn't make them any less firemen than the ones that just waggle hoses at the flames, Lil."

Ayla watched the exchange intently.

"If we'd had more of the waggling hose ones in this town, Bernard, I might still have a house," she snapped back at him. "You can't pray away every issue facing Cassandra, you know."

"Maybe *you* can't," Serena Bliss hissed under her breath at the mayor.

It was two hours later when the three of us left the bungalow. I looked around for Archie, but couldn't find him anywhere. He must have gone off to get something to eat again.

"That is the oddest meeting I have ever had in my entire life with anyone," Emma said as the we walked onto the sidewalk. "I mean, I've certainly run into your average, everyday psychic people lately...but the mayor and her guru friend over there? Those two are on another level."

There were many words spoken in the interview, but very little information. It was clear that the mayor was frightened someone targeted her, but she couldn't say why she was frightened of it, or why someone might have targeted her, no matter how many ways we asked. Serena Bliss, pious as anyone I'd ever met, spoke much and said little.

The guru simply chain-smoked through the entire meeting.

"Something is wrong here," Ayla said. "Like, I can't put my finger on it, but it was almost like the guru guy had multiple personality disorder. Like, he kept changing. It was so weird. And what was with that smoking?"

"The mayor—and Serena, too—seem more concerned that the Halloween festival takes place than finding out what happened with the house," I replied. "I just don't get it. This town does go all out for Halloween, and they do try and give the tourists what they want, and I get that's important from a financial perspective. But why do they seem so sure one has to do with the other? Nothing they said indicates any kind of link other than the coincidental timing. The house isn't even in the center of town. It's out by the lake."

Emma glanced over her shoulder at the cottage. Then, she added, "Whatever we learned, my main takeaway was that he's not too upset about the mayor losing her house. He didn't seem to care at all."

"The guru? Yeah, I caught that, too," Ayla said.

"And whatever he's acting like right now," I said, "the entire town thinks he's the bee's knees as far as I know—"

"The mayor sure doesn't," Emma pointed out. "And Serena? I had a lot of trouble pegging exactly what her deal was. Like, one minute she was genuflecting and the next she seemed annoyed."

I glanced back and added, "There must be a story behind their dislike of one another, and they didn't tell us what that was. You're right, though; he wasn't upset. And yet she's here in his bungalow, hiding from the town." I had an odd feeling about the whole situation and an even more bizarre feeling that we still weren't through with the local politics of it all. "Ayla, any ghosts?"

She shook her head. "No. I don't see anyone."

"Not even anyone you know?"

"Nope."

Emma was tapping something on her phone. "Well, the fire department is downtown taking lunch," she announced. "Let's go and ask them what they know. Maybe we'll get more out of them than Thornton implied."

CHAPTER SIX

The gravel crunched under our feet, and the heat was almost unbearable as we marched down the road. Each of us quietly contemplated the last two hours of information—which, as I mentioned, wasn't much information to go on. "You know, the more I think about it, the more I realize I learned more about this place from what those people didn't say than what they did say."

"I agree." As Emma rounded the corner, she stopped abruptly and glanced at a large open barn across the street. "But here's a question. Why would Lillian Thornton ask for outside help if she wasn't going to be forthcoming? Do you think she invited us here as a prop in whatever political garbage is going on between her and the guru? Could that be all this is?"

"What do you mean by prop?" Ayla asked.

"Astra?" As soon as I heard my name called, I turned around and saw Jason Bishop staring at me, his eyes wider and more expansive than I'd ever seen them, as he came out of a yogurt shop. "What are you and Ayla doing here?" Jason looked over at the detective. "Emma, wasn't it? We met at the marathon, yes?" He held out his hand, and they shook.

"The mayor of Cassandra asked for help from the Forkbridge Police Department to investigate a house fire last night that may—or may not—be arson," I told Jason. "Emma and I got assigned, and we brought Ayla over because she has some abilities that might come in handy if we run into the ghosts that are supposed to infest this town. Why are you here?"

Jason looked surprised. "Really? Ayla, I didn't know you could see ghosts."

"I can only see them when they're actually in front of me, and there are no ghosts here. In fact, it's kind of weird. There are fewer ghosts here than there are in Forkbridge. It's like they all went away or decided to leave at the same time."

"So what are you doing in Cassandra in the

middle of a workday?" I asked again. It's possible that I came across as a little too eager to learn the specifics, a little sharper than I intended. "I just thought you'd be at the school teaching, that's all," I added, my voice softer.

"My mother is the mayor of Cassandra and the owner of the house." To my credit, I kept my jaw from dropping and cracking the sidewalk. "I received a call from her this morning, informing me of the fire that occurred last night. My mother, who is not particularly adept at paperwork, enlisted my assistance in processing her insurance claims. There's a sub teaching my class," Jason said. "As for what I'm doing right here? This place has delicious croissant sandwiches, and I grabbed one for lunch."

I didn't care about the croissants. I was still reeling from the revelation this was Mayor Pink Sarong's son. "Your mother is Lillian Thornton?" I asked.

Ayla's mouth fell open as if she just caught what he was saying. "Yeah, hold on a sec. The woman we just met in the guru's house with the pink sarong? That's your mom?" When he nodded, she frowned. "But you don't have the same last name."

"My parents divorced when I was about four

years old." Jason was unmoved by the question, and there were no signs of an internal conflict in his body language. "I talk to my father pretty infrequently, and that's been the case ever since he left. He's an anthropology professor at Harvard." Jason shrugged. "I don't think he could cope with the idea of a kid, and I don't think my mother really had the energy to force the issue."

Jason's openness was surprising. He had no qualms about spilling the beans to people he barely knew. It's not something I'd ever think of doing.

Jason was nothing like me.

Maybe even the complete opposite of me.

Just saying.

I worked to keep the thoughts from showing on my face, but as if he read them clear in my eyes, he added, "Oh yeah, I'm an only child, too. In case you were curious." Then he winked at me, following it with a soft smile.

I kept my gaze on him and tried to ignore the wink.

And the soft smile.

"How about the house? Did you get it taken care of?"

Jason looked away to greet an elderly gray-haired woman who had appeared out of nowhere.

She returned the wave and took a step toward the curb; as soon as Jason realized she was attempting to cross the street, he rushed over and offered to assist her.

"Okay, that's hot," Emma whispered. "Smoking sexy hot. Look at that."

I rolled my eyes.

"Don't roll your eyes at me. How are you not dating this guy yet, Astra? He's everything you said you wanted. He fits all the criteria you've ever mentioned. He's available, and he seems to be interested in you, too."

"I know, right?" Ayla grumbled.

Jason turned around and headed back. I only had time for a glare and a quick, "Shut up, both of you."

"Sorry about that," Jason said cheerfully. "Mrs. Stamper has cataracts, and I didn't want her to get hurt. Anyway, Mom's house? Yeah, I just talked to the insurance company. She may not like dealing with bureaucracy, but she got a good policy. They're going to have somebody out to take a look later this afternoon."

"Your mother doesn't like dealing with bureaucracy?" I asked, incredulous. "She's the mayor."

"Mayors are bureaucracy, right? I mean, like, that's their whole job." Ayla asked me.

"Mom's an ambitious go-getter that wants to change the world," he responded with a chuckle. "She doesn't want to handle the paperwork that might entail, though."

"So, question. What do you think happened to your mother's house?" Emma asked my running partner. "Do you think it was arson?"

Before I could hear Jason's answer, my phone vibrated on my hip. I pulled it out of my pocket to read Ami's name. "I'll be right back. I have to take this." I turned away from the group and tapped the screen. "What's up?"

"Hey, I just wanted to let you know I did a reading on your arson fire thing? The five of swords keeps coming up over and over and over again," Ami said in a rush. "The five of swords! Man. I just can't believe that. In Cassandra? Who would've thought?" She paused, waiting for me to say something. When I didn't, she said, "You do know what the five of swords represents, don't you?"

"Um, a guy with some swords?" I guessed with uncertainty.

I heard the exhale of my sister's breath directly into the phone. "That's what's on the card, but I asked you if you knew what it *represented*, which, obviously, you don't," Ami told me with exasperation.

"Fundamentally, the card indicates ruthless behavior. It can be theft or armed robbery, or anything, really, involving malice. It was crossed by the seven of swords, too."

"More guys with more swords?"

"Oh, man, Astra, you really need a remedial witch class, I'm telling you. It means somebody is getting away with something."

"So, from your reading, you're guessing this was arson."

"I did a reading on it. This is not a *guess*," Ami responded, her voice slightly offended. "This is divination, Astra. Someone over there is getting away with something right now. Something they did maliciously. Since a flaming tower came up in the reading? Yeah, I would say the cards believe it's arson."

Ami's tendency to anthropomorphize her paper stock with pretty pictures always made my eyes roll.

The cards believed nothing.

They were *cards*.

Nothing more than paper with images.

But whatever power in the universe affected

those cards? Whatever animated those images to tell us a story? That power wanted us to be aware that someone roaming the streets of Cassandra had a plan—and was willing to do some nasty things to further it.

"EVERYTHING OKAY AT HOME?" Jason asked as I rejoined the group.

Was everyone psychic? "How did you know I was talking to my sister?"

"You never talk about anyone else on our runs other than family, so I assumed it was one of your sisters. Since Emma is here."

I locked my gaze on him. I was torn between ripping him a new one for his judgmental presumptuousness and being overly sweet to him in the hopes that he would provide me with information about his mother.

I chose the latter option.

I gave him the sweetest, kindest smile imaginable. "Ami did a reading on the fire at your mother's house last night. She thinks someone is doing something malicious in this town, and as of right now, they are getting away with it."

"So it was arson?" Jason asked.

"She wasn't that specific."

"Did she do the reading before or after we showed up?" Emma asked with a flamboyant hand gesture. "Because I would think she did it before we showed up. After we showed up, clearly no one is getting away with *anything*. I'm just saying."

Jason bowed toward Emma. "I'm impressed with your confidence, Detective Sullivan. If I could bottle that and give it to my students, they'd do a lot better on tests." He glanced at his watch. "If there's anything I can do to help you all, just let me know. I'm free all day."

"Where are the ghosts?" Ayla blurted out, her hands on her hips. "If the mayor is your mother, you must have been raised here in this town with the spiritualist stuff, right? So you would know how many spirits are usually here." My younger sister shook her head, her arms crossed over her chest, her face flushed with exasperation. "Where are they? I haven't seen anyone all morning."

Jason smiled and eased the tension. "Didn't you three just come from the guru's house?"

"How'd you know that?" I asked suspiciously.

Jason pointed at Emma. "She just told me."

Oh.

"Anyway," Jason said returning his gaze to

Ayla. "What did he tell you about where the ghosts have gone?"

"We didn't ask. They told me not to talk during the interviews, and they didn't think to say anything." Ayla glared at Emma, her eyes filled with resentment. "So, now it's up to you. Just tell me."

"This is still kind of an interview, you know," I told Ayla as her face turned bright pink. "Emma has a reason for asking what she asks and for not asking what she doesn't ask. If you really want to get into law enforcement, I would suggest you observe and contemplate why she does what she does."

"Yeah, actually, I just forgot," Emma said with a shrug. "It didn't have anything directly to do with the fire."

"Right, and I'm the one that should keep quiet? Of course it's related! Oh, my gosh!" my sister shouted at the detective. "You people are so frustrating! I don't know how you solve anything!"

"That's not really the way to prove you should be more involved, Ayla," Jason told my sister without judgment. "I've had lots of kids like you in my class, and you know what? Eventually, they see the sharp edges aren't necessary. You always catch far more flies with honey than you do with vinegar."

Our disapproval didn't seem to bother the youngster. "I don't like flies, and I do not act like a mean girl!" If looks could kill, my sister's would have had Jason skewered seconds later.

"You do, a little bit. Or, at least, you have been lately," I said to Ayla with the utmost authority I could muster. She glared. "What? More barbs you'd like to fling? You do remember we had a deal about your behavior on this little field trip."

"You know—"

"I have an idea, though I might regret it," Emma interjected, her voice cutting off whatever Ayla was getting ready to say next. She took in a deep breath and looked Jason up and down. "You know this town better than we do. We hoped Ayla would get us some information about who was who and what was what, but with the ghosts nowhere to be found, we're at a bit of a disadvantage. You want to be our Cassandra chaperon?"

Jason half-heartedly pushed his tussled brown hair out of his face. "Like, right this second?" He looked a little surprised.

"You have anything better to do? You just offered help. Was that just you being polite?"

Emma asked, her face without expression. She glanced around at the rest of us. "What? Can you think of a better idea?"

"I feel like this is starting to become some weird experiment on your part—add witch, add thirteen-year-old, add middle school teacher." I glanced around the town street and thought about it for a few seconds. Finally, I nodded. "You are right. We need information, and nobody is giving it up. So, Jason, you've volunteered yourself as a tour guide for the day."

"Um. Yeah. I didn't really expect you to take me up on it, but okay." He laughed nervously and shook his head. "I know the town, but I don't know anything about police investigations." Jason cleared his throat and looked at me. "If you don't know where to ask about what you need to know, how am I supposed to help you?"

Despite my agreeing to this, the voice of reason in my head wanted to slap Emma silly. She could have asked the mayor or the guru for help and didn't. I suspected her request of Jason was half because it was useful and half because she thought I should've gone out on a date with him a long time ago.

Nothing Emma'd said so far even convinced

me she thought there was a crime here to investigate.

"First, we're going over to the fire house." Emma pointed down the street. "I want to talk to the firemen."

"The fire men?" Jason frowned. "You mean the sacred fire keepers?"

"Is that the closest thing you people have to a fire department?" Jason nodded. "Then that's what I mean."

UPON ENTERING what appeared to be an abandoned warehouse, Jason introduced us to what passed for a fire department in Cassandra, Florida.

It was a wonder the whole place hadn't burned down years ago.

It was swarming with people huddled together around bright flames as if they were in Alaska rather than Florida in the fall.

"These are the sacred fire keepers of Cassandra," Jason announced.

Directly in front of us was a black wrought-iron stand with eight candles, each of which was approximately two feet in height. Prior to speaking with anyone else in the building, Jason lit a single candle.

Three of the men turned to face him and greeted him by name as soon as the flame burst brightly into the air. "Edgar," Jason called back. "How are you? Willis? You look wonderful. How have you been?"

"What did you say?" asked Edgar, motioning toward his ear. The man's skin was pale, his gray hair cut short, and he dressed in a gray robe. The strong scent of incense and camphor poured off him, The scent was heavy, like the smell you'd get if you used an entire tube of Ben-Gay in one sitting.

Not that I would know.

"I said 'how are you?'" replied Jason, his voice louder.

"Did you say anything before that?" asked Edgar.

"Yeah," said Jason, practically shouting, "I said your name."

"Oh," Edgar hollered. "Sorry. The fire spirit usually amplifies what people say here so that my hearing loss isn't a problem. But, unfortunately, since all the spirits left town a few days ago, I've been having a hard time." Now that he was closer, I could see he was a hard, sinewy man. His hands were rough-skinned, calloused like a laborer's.

The ghosts left a few days ago...right before Halloween?

"Where did they go?" I asked.

"What?" Edgar shouted at me. Then he pointed at his ears. "Can't hear ya!"

"Edgar tried to get into explosion prayer when he was younger," Jason said without seeming the least bit alarmed at the concept of prayer via explosive device. "Unfortunately, he didn't master it fast enough to save his hearing."

As I watched Jason introduce us to all these things that resembled magic—but that this town was adamant were not, in any way, magic—I suddenly realized why he'd never been particularly alarmed or concerned I was rumored to be a witch.

Clearly, he grew up with the paranormal—even if these people called it prayer.

And used explosives.

"Did you know Jason was from here?" Ayla whispered, as Edgar and my running partner continued shouting a casual conversation at one another. "He never said anything about it, did he?"

Before I could answer, all hell broke loose.

"Wait a minute. I know you! That's a witch!" Edgar yelled at me, pointing. He looked horrified, and his mouth moved as if he wanted to say something but couldn't. After a short pause gaping like a fish, he added, "And not just any witch! That hag has the uniform of Satan's army!"

That's twice in one day.

Jason nodded calmly. "Edgar, she is a witch, but she's here to help—"

"Of course it is. We need to kill it!" Edgar said it with such force that his eyeballs nearly popped out of his head. His face was flushed with rage and fear, his skin almost the color of fake Halloween blood. "Willis, we gotta kill—"

The man slapped Edgar. "I can't believe you would even suggest that, brother!" he yelled. Willis appeared to wait for a response, and when he didn't get the one he wanted, he slapped Edgar across the face again. "We are guardians! Protectors, not destroyers! Never forget that."

"What?" Edgar asked, his expression confused, his hand against his face.

Willis glared and scowled at the shorter man. "I said you're a moron!"

"Okay, this place is even crazier than I thought it was going to be," Emma told me with a glee that was entirely inappropriate to the situation. She stepped forward and raised her voice. "Edgar, as a reminder—I work as a detective for the police department. Please do not attempt to assassinate the police consultant. I'll have to put you in jail. I don't want to have to take you into custody." She glanced at Willis. "That goes for assault, too. Let's dial all that back, shall we?"

"You people are here about the mayor's house fire?" Willis asked. His eyes flared in surprise. "Even that kid?"

I nodded. "We're investigating it, trying to determine the cause."

"Well, we *know* the cause," Willis told me definitively, the big man crossing his arms. "Could have saved you a trip from Forkbridge if you'd just picked up the phone and called." The other men in the room slowly gathered around us in a semicircle, nodding and murmuring their quiet agreement.

"Well, we're here now. What do you believe the cause of the fire was?" Emma asked him.

"The mayor's dating the police captain over in Forkbridge. I would've thought you knew that. It's your boss," he explained with a shrug. "It is against the spirits' wishes for us to have personal relationships with outsiders, and what better example of this than the mayor sleeping with a police captain from the cursed town next door?" He made a sound that sounded like a half chuckle. "We're pretty sure fire spirits burned her house down when she didn't stop."

"And that's funny?" I asked, appalled.

He shrugged. "Well, it's not un-funny. She was warned."

So much for his role as protector. "Who warned her to stop?"

Willis looked at me like I was dumb. "Well, the guru did, obviously. Who else would do it? He speaks for the spirits."

"I thought the spirits spoke for themselves?" Ayla asked suspiciously.

"Nah, not anymore. Not since the change about a month ago."

That's when we realized there was a lot more going on in Cassandra than met the eye.

CHAPTER SEVEN

The other fire men (and they were all men) appeared to be uncomfortable as Willis extended his hand toward a bench on the far side of the room. He was preparing to tell us the story of how things had changed.

The bench had a curved metal surface that looked like a long sofa with a blackish sheen to it. It looked like a missile…

…or a very fat coffin.

Despite the fact that we moved in that direction, none of us sat down.

"Why do you look like someone just kicked your cat, Joe?" Willis asked, noticing the deep frown on one of the fire men's face. "It's not like this is a secret."

"It may not be a secret, *Will*, but we don't normally go around telling witches our business, do we?" Joe turned his head in my direction, his frown morphing into a phony smile. "No offense meant."

Despite his best efforts to appear friendly, it was clear that he wasn't. The glint in his eyes told a story all by itself.

"No, that's true; we don't normally go and tell witches our business. But we do put it in a newsletter and give it out over at the Piggy Pickle Shack on Main Street to anyone that wants to read about it." Willis pointed his blunt finger at Joe. "Now, should I make them go read the newsletter from a month ago, or should I just tell them?"

Joe glared and glanced at a short blond man with eyes like arctic ice. He was wiry and lean with eyelids hung low above his canny eyes.

"Tell us what?" Emma asked.

"About a month ago, some of the elders got together and decided the younger psychics were misusing their ties to the ghosts," said Willis with a slow shake of his head. "Regrettable stuff. Kids today just don't have the same respect that we were brought up with. They don't listen to their elders, and they all want a quick way of getting fame or fortune—"

"Or the answers on an SAT test," one man grumbled.

The others nodded their heads.

"You see, people that can actually talk to the spirits are expected to do something with that tie. Value it. Hold it sacred. You don't just get that ability for no reason. If you have it, you have responsibilities—to the ghosts and to the community." Ayla nodded in agreement. "Since the next generation wasn't acting responsibly, the leadership put a stop to their ability to talk to the spirit world whenever they wanted."

Jason Bishop appeared to be taken aback. A line of brilliantly white, perfectly straight teeth appeared when his mouth dropped open, and his rapid blinking revealed his surprise.

"Did you know about this?" Emma asked Jason. "I'm assuming from your expression this is the first you've heard of it."

"No. I mean, yes. I mean, that's surprising," Jason said. "That they did it, not that this is the first I heard of it. Because it is." Jason had been completely thrown off his rocker by Will's statement, and his words were coming out in a jumbled muddle. "Mom and I don't talk about what's going on with the town too much. I don't live here anymore, so I guess she doesn't really see much of a need to keep me in the loop."

I turned back to Willis. "What do you mean 'put a stop' to their ability?" There were many ways that could have been done, but most involved magic or magical items. (Which, as I've pointed out, I think these people use. They just don't want to *admit* it to themselves or anyone else.) "How did you stop them from being able to talk to ghosts?"

"I'm a fire tender, so I didn't put a stop to anything. That's not my job." Edgar passed a note over to Willis. The fire tender read it, folded it up, and put it back in his pocket. "Not a problem," Willis murmured. Then, turning back to us, he said, "I'm not one of the elders. So I can't tell you how any of that was done. Not something I'm familiar with. I'd have to check with my committee on that issue."

I stared at Will's pocket.

As if she heard my stare, Ayla's head snapped up and followed my gaze. Catching her eye again, I reached out casually and tapped the area just above my right breast.

She stuck her hand in her pocket and wiggled

her fingers through the fabric, raising her eyebrow in question.

I dropped my head slightly in as unobtrusive a nod as I could manage.

No words were needed as she looked back at him, narrowed her eyes, and plotted the teleport theft.

"So, who are the elders?" I asked Will. "Is it a group? Are there elections? How does that work?"

"Well, I thought that would be obvious. The mayor, the guru, and Serena Bliss, their assistant. That's it. Just three. We're a small community; we don't need many more people than that."

It appeared Ayla was aimlessly wandering around the room, looking at the various candles and flames—she was really searching for an out-of-the-way spot to teleport the note. A place where she would not be easily noticed by the fire men.

"Well, Bill Platt is the leader of the Merchants Guild, so he's kind of a junior elder," the short man with blond hair told Will. "We have the guilds, so there are other leaders. But they don't get a vote. If they had, it maybe wouldn't have happened." I raised my eyebrow. "Bill's been pretty angry at the mayor going on months now.

For all sorts of things." The man's square jaw and broad shoulders were accented by a pair of slanted eyebrows and a stern expression.

"For what sorts of things, Mr..." I held out my hand, silently asking for his name.

"My name is Robert," he responded curtly and then glanced at Jason with cold indifference. "You can just call me Robert. And Bill's had it in for the mayor ever since she forbid anyone to buy gas cars. She wants to make gas-powered cars completely illegal in the town. Still, Bill was able to argue against that because it would affect tourism."

"She forbid everyone, or she passed a law?" I asked him.

The fire tenders laughed. The short man with the ice blue eyes—Robert the stern—smirked back at Will, who nodded.

"There's not much of a difference here," Will said.

Robert nodded.

"So, anyway, to get back to the original point? The elders cut off everyone's connection with the ghosts unless you ask their permission. The psychics have to go to the guru to get their ghost for readings. Then, when done, they have to return them."

Wait a minute.

They have to return a ghost?

Return.

A *ghost*.

Spirits were not the same as library books. They were people, they just didn't have physical bodies. Unlike on-demand movies or rental cars, you didn't check them out and check them back in. Despite the fact that they are dead, they are fully formed independent people with "lives."

I tried to keep my judgment to myself, but I was worried that my disgust was spreading across my face. "Return them to where? Where are they?"

Robert and Edgar were looking at each other with weird expressions I happened to catch out of the corner of my eye.

"I'm not an elder, ma'am. I don't know how they do what they do. I just know they did, and that was the end of it," Will shrugged. "I just tend the fire. I keep it burning where it's supposed to be, and I put it out when it's not supposed to be there."

Edgar's lips were set in a tight line.

"MAN, and I thought Forkbridge was weird," Emma said as we walked out of the fire house. "All these years, people have been telling me this place is filled with crazy cultists, and I never believed it. I thought people in our town were just intolerant bigots." The detective leaned against a lamp post half a block from the fire house building and looked back. "I'm starting to wonder if I was wrong all these years. This feels like a low-level "Children of the Corn" rip-off."

"Now, wait a minute," Jason said, his voice holding some slight offense. "I'll admit that exchange in there was out of the ordinary even for Cassandra. Our folks do get a little bit weird around Halloween, but that doesn't make it a cult. Cults don't let people leave. I'm the mayor's son, and I was able to move to Forkbridge, go to college, and become a teacher. No one is forced to stay."

"Can you talk to spirits?" I asked him curiously.

"No, but I don't see what that has to do with—"

"Maybe that's why you were allowed to leave. Have you ever known a death speaker that left? Anyone you know just book out with their second antenna into the great beyond to go become a plumber or something?"

Jason frowned. "I know you call it that, but that's not what we call it. But no, I'm not a medium."

"So it's 'we' now, is it?" I asked with a raised eyebrow. "How very cult-y."

He had a pitying expression on his face when he looked at me.

"Ignore her, Jason. Do you think the fire ghost or whatever set your mother's house on fire?" Emma asked Jason point-blank. "You grew up here. You were raised with these beliefs. Does their explanation makes sense to you?"

"I don't know. They have beliefs that I'd never be taught since I wasn't chosen to be a fire tender," Jason said, "but we can't rule it out. They looked like they believed it."

"No, they looked like they were hiding something," I told him.

Ayla raised her hand. Emma nodded and gestured for her to speak up.

"If the ghosts were put under some kind of control a month ago, then if the ghosts started the fire, they didn't do it on their own," Ayla said. "You heard what they said in there. Everyone in town has to check them out of some kind of ghost library. So, like, I think they're blaming the ghosts to cover up for someone else. Maybe. If it wasn't an accident."

"She's got a point. Blaming ghosts is a very convenient excuse for any of these townspeople with a grudge against the mayor," I added. "Especially if that's the closest thing this place has to a fire department. Anyone who's met those people would know there was no way they were going to put out a raging house fire at the edge of town."

"I haven't seen any other ghosts or heard any other ghosts," Ayla said. "We haven't found any other signs of a ghost anywhere. So I think they're just blaming them because they know that you're a police officer, and you'll just drop it if that's what happened. I mean, you can't arrest a ghost."

Emma grimaced. "They don't know me very well. Ghost perp or not, I want to know why this happened, not just who did it. My Spidey-sense tells me someone is lying about what's going on here."

"To tell you the truth, that's likely why my mother asked for Captain Harmon's help," Jason said with a brief smile. "She needs to know the why of this, not just the who."

"Especially considering Ami's reading," Emma said with a nod.

"So, let's say it's not a ghost curse. We have a bunch of problems with this case. We haven't found any other evidence of arson. We can't figure out why the house caught fire. We won't unless we hire a forensic investigator or I stick my hands in a fire to read the ruins. We expected the ghosts to tell us the story—or at least give us some clues." I held up my hands. "No ghosts."

When I looked over, Jason was staring at me intently. He looked at me for a moment before quickly averting his gaze. I was immediately uncomfortable, though I wasn't sure if it was because he was staring at me or trying to conceal his expression.

He must've been feeling awkward as well because he asked, "So, did anyone see that note that Edgar handed Will?"

"Yeah, I did! I—"

Jason held up his hand and cut Ayla off. "Edgar never left the group while we were talking. No one called; no one came in. Edgar wanted to tell Will something without us being aware of what they were talking about, like an eighth-grader passing notes in class. It had to be about—"

"Astra!" Ayla shouted, waving her fist with the piece of paper. "It was about Astra. Well, at least I think it was. She was talking to Will when Edgar passed it to him. So the her has to be her, right?" Ayla was so excited that she forgot that none of us had the first clue what she was talking about.

"You got the note?" Emma asked, pulling herself off the lamppost.

Ayla nodded.

"How?"

"I am a girl of many, many talents, I told you!" Ayla unfolded the paper and handed it to the detective. Emma reached out to take it, then quickly changed her mind. "What's the matter? They won't even know how I got it."

"So, technically, you stole that," Emma told her.

"It's just paper."

"*Stolen* paper."

Ayla shrugged. "Technically, those men might've set the mayor's house on fire." She held out the paper with a triumphant look on her face. "Just take it. It's just a note. I bet you've never arrested anyone for stealing a piece of paper."

Emma glanced over at me. "Can you?"

I nodded and took the paper from Ayla. Then,

unfolding it carefully, I read three hen-scratched words.

DON'T TELL HER.

NOTHING SAYS conspiracy quite like a note from one person to another, instructing the other not to tell you about something they both know.

I wasn't convinced that the fire tenders were responsible for the crime. Heck, I wasn't even sure there had been a crime. Nonetheless, I was beginning to realize that if someone had committed a crime like arson, they would almost certainly require the assistance of members of the fire tender group in order to cover it up.

If that was their intention, anyway.

While the detective continued to interrogate Ayla about her teleportation abilities, I summoned Jason to my side. With the stare and the revelations of the day, I was taken aback by the fact that Jason and I had been running together for months and he'd never told me about his ties to the spiritualists (which meant he'd *always* been aware of my identity and never said a word).

The two of us sat next to each other on a park

bench along the sidewalk, and I struggled how to start the conversation. Jason looked down, as if expecting something. "Let me guess. You have questions."

I sighed. "Yeah. I have questions."

"Shoot."

I started with a friendly, non-confrontational, "So, Cassandra is your hometown, is it?" But without letting him respond, I launched into a barrage of follow-ups. "Is this the reason you've never asked me about the witch stuff, or the magic stuff, and why you seem to know more about all that stuff than a normal human being should know?"

"Two sentences, five questions," he laughed. "Impressive."

I think I blushed. "Sorry."

"As far as me being normal, this is central Florida, Astra. So what's normal anyway?" Jason gave me a sideways glance I sensed more than I saw. "I didn't go out of my way to hide anything from you. My hometown, your family—those things may inform who we are, but they aren't who we are. You know what I mean?" I turned to look at him. "I grew up with certain expectations that I chose to defy. That wasn't easy."

"No, I hear that," I agreed.

"I just don't volunteer that information." Jason paused. "You didn't either, you know."

He got me there. I didn't respond.

"Will wasn't wrong about one thing, by the way. People here are expected to date within the community. Those of us that go outside of it, we are not looked upon with much...pride or affection."

My head snapped up. "Wait a minute. Who said anything about dating?" I asked. I raised my eyes to the sky and scanned the treetops in case we were about to be dive-bombed by an interfering owl.

But there was nothing there.

"I meant about my mom, Astra." Jason met my eyes and grinned. "The fire tenders brought up her dating Captain Harmon. I was just confirming what they said. I wasn't implying anything."

He looked more amused than he should have been.

My heart was pounding a little—because of the heat—and I tried to change the subject. "People seem to be pretty fond of you even though you left. You don't seem to be any the worse for having moved out, gone to college, and now working in the world outside of this town."

He smiled again and tossed his head. "No, you're right, that's true. For now, anyway. I haven't married someone outside the community yet. If I had, I wouldn't have been quite as much help to you today."

Why do we keep coming back to dating and marriage?

The sun dipped behind an afternoon rain cloud, and the street suddenly darkened. I was grateful for the small break in the sunshine as my skin cooled. "Marrying outside the group is the ultimate sin, huh?" I asked.

"I don't know that I would call it a sin. But, it does seem to be considered an uncrossable line, a choice you don't come back from." Jason seemed to have a sense of peace about his decision, the future memory of the outsider wife he was sure he would have one day. He lowered his voice and added, "My mother and Captain Harmon? They have been seeing each other for the past few months, and from what Mom has told me, it's pretty serious."

I raised my eyebrow. "Uncrossable line serious?"

"Maybe," he admitted. "He makes her really happy. I think if they asked her to give up being mayor for him, she probably would."

My mind was tickled by his statement, and a nostalgic image of my mother's lessons on the spiritualists at Cassandra popped into my head. I'm not sure what possessed me to think of that. I saw the class in my mind's eye and suddenly remembered.

While the mayor was an elected position, that position was usually held by the most talented, most renowned psychic in the town.

"Your mom is a heck of a psychic, isn't she?" I asked to confirm.

Jason nodded. "She can call ghosts from anywhere in the world, even from alternate realms. At least that's what the guru claimed—the alternate realms thing. She seems to know, without asking, what people come to her for, and has the strongest connection to the spirit world of anyone in her generation." He looked proud of his mother, proud of her talent. "People wait months for an appointment with her."

And for that, she had a gigantic house on Witch Lake.

A home far from the center of town, far from the tourists. A place that gave her solace and peace and quiet. Isolation. A respite the most potent psychic in Cassandra would need. "Where

is she staying now that her house burned down?"
I asked…

…even though it seemed clear that she was
staying—unhappily—in the bungalow with guru
grabby-hands.

"She has to stay with the guru for the next
week," Jason explained as he pointed to the
Halloween celebration decorations. "She can only
stay with the elders during Halloween, or in her
own home."

I raised my eyebrow.

"I know, it sounds ridiculous, but it's
tradition. See, we believe the elders get extremely
taxed during the Halloween season. So they stay
close to one another to shore up each other's
powers. It's supposed to make sure we don't miss
communication from an important spirit. What if
Lincoln or Washington showed up and, like,
everyone was napping?"

"Abraham Lincoln?" He nodded. "Your town is
concerned Abraham Lincoln might pop by, and
everyone would be napping?"

He looked down sheepishly. "I know, it
sounds weird. Anyway, usually, they stay at
Mom's house since she had the most room and it
was the most out of the way. Personally? I suspect
it's really about self-protection. Halloween can

get crazy, and some tourists can be overly enthusiastic."

Now instead of staying at Witch Lake, they were staying in a small one-room bungalow in the center of town. In the middle of all the festivities.

That seemed…a strange coincidence.

Would someone really burn down her house just to get her closer to town for Halloween? It didn't make sense.

No, that couldn't be the reason.

Could it?

And yet…

The mayor's home burned down, but she and her dog are safe. Just not any of her stuff. Just not her house. That—her house—was flattened into a big, charbroiled pancake.

I sighed.

Emma was right. This place was just weird.

CHAPTER EIGHT

*E*mma sighed watching Jason and Ayla examine something across the street. "This isn't going to be a walk in the park, is it?"

I looked around the festively decorated town square hoping I could spot some kind of magic answer. "I feel like until we figure out why the ghosts are missing or someone talks, we're just spinning our wheels. Something big is going on in this town. But I can't put my finger on what it is. Or who's doing it. Or if it's even any of our business, really."

"So, question."

"Shoot."

"Why didn't you just take off your gloves and read the embers of the house when we were out at the property this morning?" Emma didn't sound accusatory. Just genuinely curious. "You mentioned reading the ruins. I don't get why you didn't."

"Fire cleanses," I told her. "Flames are used in nature as part of a purification process. It has real benefits, but some drawbacks. When a fire burns through a region, the grass in the surrounding area will flourish as a result of the scorching, right? It's time to say goodbye to the old and hello to the new and improved. New nutrients have been introduced to the soil. It *appears* to be destructive—and it is—but it is destructive for a specific reason with a good outcome." I paused. "It's also transformative. It changes things, including what I can get psychically."

Emma glanced at me in surprise. "Wait a minute. You can't read something that's been burned? Like, at all?"

I looked at her for a moment. "Can't is a strong word. Let's just say reading something that's been burned to a crisp is not the most reliable method of psychometry I have in my arsenal. The element—fire—is associated with change, destruction, and renewal, but I look for things to read that *haven't* changed much." I turned and held up my hands. "As with all psychic abilities, accuracy may vary."

The detective nodded.

Across the street, an elementary school-age boy who'd been walking down the road stopped and stared at Jason and Ayla, his jaw dropping in surprise. With a loud whoop, I watched the slightly chubby young man run in a beeline for Jason, launch himself at the teacher, and wrap his arms around him.

Jason laughed and gave the enthusiastic young man a hug back.

"I think it's safe to say that everyone adores Jason Bishop except for you," she said, her tone smug.

"You got into a lot of trouble as a kid for not thinking before you talked, didn't you? You should really come with a warning label." I didn't want to talk about Jason Bishop and adoration. "He's a friend. We run together. I don't dislike him."

"But?"

"But nothing. Don't worry about me. Worry about your eyebrows. They're probably the reason that you don't have a boyfriend and are constantly obsessed with whether I do." Emma made a face as if she was deeply hurt by my knock against her permanently unshaped eyebrows, and then she chuckled. "Besides, that owl isn't going to let me date."

"Archie?" Her smile faded. "What do you mean?"

"The prince of Cassandra over there was on the verge of asking me on a date this morning," I said with some annoyance. "Archie decided the best way to dissuade him from his intentions was a raptor attack to the face."

The detective gasped, "Oh my gosh! He did not."

"He did." I expected her to object to his attack, make a snarky comment, something. But, instead, she watched the three across the street for a while and then asked quietly, "Another question. Do you think your goddess doesn't want you with a man, and that's why he did it?" I blinked. "I remember a little bit about Athena from mythology, and man-hating is probably generous."

"Athena was a feminist," I responded instantly. "While cultural musings going back eons insinuate man-hating is a pre-requisite to feminism, that's not actually the case. She sided with men multiple times in her myths. And, to be frank, she leveraged the male power structure." I glanced over at Emma's knowing gaze. "Not that she exists. The myths, I mean."

"Right. The myths." There was bright sarcasm in Emma's voice.

"What is that supposed to mean?"

Emma drank deeply from a water bottle, thrust the top back on it, and raised her sloppy, bushy eyebrow. "You realize you are a myth to the majority of the world's population, don't you? However, you and I both understand that, while the majority of people believe you are a myth, you are not. So it's possible—just possible—that the goddess Athena isn't either."

I looked across the darkening street and watched Jason, my running partner. His broad smile was genuine as he conversed with the Cassandran boy. The youngster talked non-stop, his hands waving in all directions as he spoke. Ayla's excitement was palpable as she listened to Jason and the boy. I sighed. "No one knows the truth about anybody, Emma. Or the real truth about anything. Not really."

"You're a walking, talking paradox, Astra. A magical being that doesn't believe in anything she can't see," Emma said and laughed. Then, suddenly, she stopped abruptly and frowned.

"What?"

"Cynical people like you are the reason God doesn't talk to us anymore, you know," Emma told me flatly.

AYLA'S FACE WAS GLOWING, energized even, as the three ran back across to where Emma and I stood by the car. Well, Ayla ran. The other two walked. "Jason introduced me to Melvin Platt," she said, pointing back toward the pair. "He's the same age as me, and he's homeschooled, too!" Ayla looked like she could burst with glee; I could tell she was charmed by the boy.

"Is he, now?" I smiled, though my stomach seized up a little. Ayla's excitement at making a new friend was untouched by the realization that my mother would never allow her to maintain this tie with a Cassandran. The explosive fight destined to ensue over Melvin might well be epic. "I guess that's why he's not in school, either."

"He has to help his dad prepare the gas station for all the visitors that come in for Halloween. Did you know that all the stores decorate for Halloween? There's nowhere in this whole town that doesn't give out candy. Isn't that cool?" My sister's explanation was breathlessly cheerful, and it gave me an instant sense memory of my own childhood—the jealousy I felt that other kids could celebrate the holiday so associated with what I was, and I couldn't. "Are we going to still be investigating on Halloween? Will we have to get costumes to blend in?"

"If she really wants to go, I bet we could stretch this out accidentally on purpose," Emma said with a smile.

"No," I said.

"Yes!" Ayla shouted simultaneously.

"You can't go trick-or-treating in Cassandra." My resolve was unwavering.

"You can't go trick-or-treating in Cassandra." Ayla mimicked my tone and then gave me a condescending look. "But we can use Halloween in our investigation. Maybe it is about Halloween! You said it could be. We could stake out the gas station with Melvin, see all the comings and goings!"

"No," I repeated firmly.

"Yes!"

"No!"

"Yes!"

"I said no," I told her pointedly. "And don't make that face at me." My sister crossed her arms in stony defiance. I turned toward Emma. "See what you did? Give an inch, and she's already running three days ahead in a Halloween costume. I bet we haven't even reached the entire mile she's planning on trying to take."

Emma leaned in toward me and whispered, "What's the harm?"

Before I could answer, Jason and Melvin joined us. Jason took one look at the storm of fury on Ayla's face and raised an eyebrow. "Everything okay? Something happen?"

"No," I told him.

"Yes, she doesn't want us to go to the Halloween festival!" Ayla told Jason as if she were tattling on a fellow student.

"Ayla, that's enough," I told her sternly. She was aware of what we were here to do, and I wasn't thrilled that she decided to take advantage of a serious investigation.

My sister threw her arms to her sides and planted her feet as her mouth dropped open in disbelief at what she had just heard. "You're not the—"

"Don't pull that with me," I snapped before she could finish the thought. "You know the rules. Was that whole kneeling to Mom thing just for show?"

Melvin blinked. "Wow. Dude. You kneel to

your mom?" The boy was as exuberant as ever as he spoke, his hands still flailing wildly. "You guys are even weirder than my dad said."

"If you two are busy with the investigation, Astra, I'd be happy to take her with me." Without thinking about the consequences, Jason dove into the pool of not-his-business and splashed around. Where's that damn owl when I actually need him to whack someone in the face with a wing? "The festival doesn't start until nightfall, and there are organized activities going on from early in the evening until the official start. It usually lasts until midnight or so. We can meet up before and after."

"Can we, now?" I asked him with icy coldness, turning my ire from my sister to Jason.

Jason didn't catch my clear warning tone, or he ignored it. "Absolutely. It's the one time of year we have a pretty large influx of outsiders, so no one would notice she was one of the Arden sisters," he said, looking back and forth between Ayla and me. "Especially if she were in costume."

"Astra!" Ayla whined. "I wanna see what it's like!"

"I'm not saying no because I want to ruin your fun, Ayla. You know that you're not allowed to attend anything in this town. That's not my rule.

That's Mom's rule. So you're asking me to get in the middle between you and Mom," I told the young woman, my face red with anger. "I can't do that."

"Mom won't even know." Ayla's voice was defiant, and her expression was one of childish pique.

I was irritated by a number of things in that moment, including my sister for putting me in this situation, my mother for raising her in the same manner as I had been raised, and myself for being a party to something I strongly opposed.

I would have sold everything I possessed magically when I was thirteen in order to attend the Halloween festival at Cassandra. It was legendary. I totally understood what she was going through.

If it was up to me, I'd let her go in a second.

But it *wasn't* up to me.

"If I could, I would, Ayla. But I can't. I'm not going to get between you and Mom. That won't help you, and it certainly won't help me." She blinked back tears, sensing the battle was lost. "And you know it. She would have a fit if she knew you were even thinking about going."

For a few moments, Ayla's eyes were wide with childish rage. She then nodded, taking a deep breath in and exhaling a massive amount of air. "I'm sorry," she apologized quietly.

"Yeah," I answered. "I know. Me, too, kid." I turned back to Jason and said, "I appreciate the thought, but I have to say no."

"That's okay, Miss Arden," Melvin interjected brightly. "Maybe someday the Ardens and us won't be so mad at each other anymore." The young man looked at Ayla with purpose—even though they'd just met. "It seems stupid to have a rule that you have to be mad at someone. I always thought, anyway."

Ayla looked back at him, her smile wide.

Then she blushed.

Uh oh.

Instead of commenting on that look, I smiled at the young man. "That's very wise, Melvin."

He nodded at me and looked once more at Ayla, flickers of mischief in his eyes. "Besides, someday, we'll be adults, and it won't matter what they say, anyway."

"Yeah, I wouldn't bet on it," my sister told the boy with an eye roll. "Astra's old, and she just admitted she's doing something she doesn't want to do just because her mommy said she has to. So that doesn't give me a lot of hope for my future."

Jason froze, the laugh clearly desperate to escape his lips.

Wisely, he held it back.

AFTER SAYING GOODBYE TO JASON, we climbed into Emma's Chevy Malibu for the ride home. The last of the day's sunlight streamed across the sky and I marveled once again at how lovely Florida sunsets could be. "Well, it was a fun day; I'll give it that. Entertaining. I'm still not convinced the fire was arson. All we have is the word of some 'fire men' who are clearly not qualified to say which way the wind is blowing, much less how a fire got started," Emma admitted. "Whatever the captain wants us to investigate? There's just not enough information."

"They talk to the flames," Ayla piped up from the back seat.

Emma looked up. "Sorry?"

"The fire tenders. They talk to the flames. That's how they do investigations. At least that's what Melvin told me," she chippered on happily, sharing information from her new friend. "He also told me that his dad has a contract with the Forkbridge Fire Department just for his gas station because he thinks the fire tender people are a bunch of whack jobs that wouldn't know a gas explosion from a UFO crash site."

"He said whack jobs?" I asked.

"Melvin? Uh-huh."

"Good job, Ayla," Emma said as she merged onto the highway. She moved over one lane, then another, and stepped on the gas. "Seems like Mr. Platt hasn't had the best experiences with city services."

"He's also not fond of Satan's hags," I reminded everyone in the car. "Granted, Melvin seems like a nice enough kid, and Platt seemed the least religious in the meeting room earlier today. But he also seemed the most intolerant." Then, suddenly, I realized something. "Hey. In that meeting, they talked about the ghosts disappearing from the town as if it was some huge mystery."

Emma frowned. "Right. And yet the fire dudes said the ghosts were taken out of rotation and had to be checked out to do readings." She tapped her fingers on the steering wheel as she went over both statements in her mind. "Huh. How did we miss that?"

"Because you weren't really taking this all that seriously," Ayla chimed in.

I turned and stared at her. "Excuse me?"

"What? You guys weren't. You seemed to think you wouldn't figure anything out pretty early on, you know. As soon as I couldn't talk to the ghosts. You kinda walked around the whole day like you were watching a reality television show or something. When I teleported that note? I was, like, the only person that really did any work."

Emma chuckled. "You weren't the only person that did work, Ayla."

"That note *was* kind of suspicious," I mused out loud.

"And you never asked about it," Ayla added. "Preconceived notions of 'nothing to see here.' You guys didn't expect to solve anything, I think."

"I beg your pardon, Miss Judgypants. You were right about one thing. We thought there would be ghosts floating all over the place you could talk to," I said.

"And to be fair, I think your sister got a bit distracted when Jason Bishop showed up," Emma said, her voice tinged with amusement.

"Unless your name is Google, stop acting like you know everything," I said.

Emma laughed.

"So, what are we doing now?" Ayla asked. "Are

we done or do we just go back tomorrow?" I could hear the hopefulness in her voice.

"Possibly. But right now, we talk to Mom and Aunt Gwennie," I responded. "As much as I hate to admit it, I don't have an explanation for what's going on in that town with the ghosts. Mom knows a lot more about Cassandra than we do. Maybe she'll have ideas about what all this means."

"She taught us everything about Cassandra, and we can't figure it out," my little sister pointed out as we pulled into Arden House's driveway.

"Mom taught us everything we know," I pointed out. I opened the car door and found myself assaulted by muggy heat and ravenous mosquitoes. "She didn't teach us everything she knows. So, let's go find out what she knows."

Emma nodded. "I also need to give Captain Harmon a ring. Even if for no other reason than to make fun of him for dating the mayor of crazy town."

CHAPTER NINE

"Again, Astra—have you two had dinner? Are you staying for a bit?" Aunt Gwennie asked.

As soon as we walked through the door, my mother approached Ayla and inquired how her day had gone. Ayla responded by telling her about Cassandra and its inhabitants and then bombarding her with questions about them. Additionally, my know-it-all younger sister was curious why I was being compensated by the Forkbridge PD for simply wandering around town and asking questions.

"I'm not paid to simply wander around and ask questions," I told her before turning to face Aunt Gwennie, who had been patiently waiting for my response. "We have not yet had dinner, ma'am, and we'd be most grateful for some food if you've made enough."

"I'll set a place for you and Emma, then." Aunt Gwennie smiled at Emma and disappeared into the kitchen.

"Kiddo, you really need to stop harassing your sister," Emma told Ayla as she set her bag by the door. "It was probably my fault that we were so sluggish in investigating the fire at the mayor's residence. I'm the police detective. She's the psychic sidekick."

When I was in the paranormal military, I was given the title of Decanus. In the Ninth Cohort, I was in charge of a group of eight legionaries. (Yeah, I know—that does not really mean anything right now.) Despite my leadership history, I accept I'm essentially Emma's right-hand man. At least with police matters.

Emma yawned and extended her arms out in front of her like a sleepy child. "So, here's the deal," she told Ayla. "We don't even know if the fire was started deliberately. Even though there is a huge amount of craziness in that town, it is not against the law to be absolutely nuts, you know. In fact, it's *almost* a requirement in central Florida. So, we took our time. Stepped lightly."

The part of myself that was still 'ass-kicking Decanus Arden of the toughest magical military ever' chafed a little bit at Emma's psychic sidekick crack.

"Sidekick, huh?"

"Oh, come on, best sidekick ever. After a few days, we'll discover that there is some sort of magical conspiracy underway, and I'll find myself serving as your sidekick. Because I won't have a clue what's going on." Emma caressed her sidearm with affection and waggled her bushy eyebrows. "Your well-armed and awesome-shot sidekick."

"I don't think there's a conspiracy." I thought about the sideways glances, whispers and secretly passed notes with warnings. "Well, let me rephrase—I don't think there's a new conspiracy. For those people, aside from the ghost thing, it appears to be just plain old regular drama." I walked into the kitchen and glanced around. "If there is a conspiracy in Cassandra, I'm almost positive it's self-made."

I pulled out two cans of Dr. Brown's Cream Soda from the fridge and tossed one to Emma before popping the top off of my own.

"Technically, all drama is self-made," Emma pointed out.

"Look, I understand why Ayla assumed we weren't putting forth much effort. We wandered around, talked to some strangers, ate stuff, and went home." I looked over my shoulder. "But I'm not sure what else we were supposed to do. Houses have been destroyed by accidental fire. Accidents happen."

"She didn't tell us much about why she thought it was arson," Emma agreed.

"She?"

"The mayor."

"Someone smelled gasoline."

Emma shrugged. "Yeah, but that's it. So, I see your point."

"Yeah, but you didn't ask her very much about why she thought it was arson," Ayla said, stepping into the kitchen from the hallway. "I mean, it was obvious that you didn't have any respect for those people at all, right?"

Emma blinked. "I don't agree with that at all."

Ayla shrugged. "You didn't like them. Either of you."

Emma raised her eyebrow. "I don't have to like people to protect and serve them. My job is to protect and serve everyone. Not just the people I like and screw everyone else."

"Those citizens who referred to us as 'Satan's

hags' in a town meeting? You're unhappy we didn't like those people?" I gave Ayla a moment to respond, but it appeared she could not think of anything to say for the first time all day. "Look, Ayla, I get what you're saying. But Emma and I didn't go to Cassandra with any preconceived notions. We were asked to investigate a fire with no assigned fire investigators." I raised my eyebrow. "There was a limited amount we could do. It was barely more than what *they* could do— which is probably why they called us in the first place."

My sister scowled and leveled an impatient look at me. "Will you at least admit the fact that the ghosts have disappeared is weird?"

I nodded. "I will admit the ghosts disappearing is weird."

"And?" she asked petulantly, a triumphant look in her eyes.

"And it's weird." The statement hung uncomfortably for a long moment as my sister stared at me. "What do you want me to say, Ayla?"

As my thirteen-year-old sister launched into me about my lackadaisical investigative skills, my mother hurriedly walked down the hall to stop her. "Astra came home to talk about the situation with her coven, Ayla." Her expression grew serious. "You know, you could definitely learn a lesson from Astra and Emma both. No one is too powerful or too knowledgeable to check in with someone else for other opinions."

Ayla opened her mouth like she might rattle off a quick comeback. Still, something made her think twice before openly challenging my mother.

"It's true, we did." I kept my tone friendly and ever so slightly deferential. "To be frank, I don't know what would cause tons of ghosts to disappear from a town known for them. Especially when there aren't any witches in the town."

"And how, pray tell, are we sure there are no witches in Cassandra?" my Aunt Gwennie asked as she stirred sauce in a pot. "Your little revolution—"

"It wasn't *my* revolution, Aunt Gwennie," I responded, reminding my aunt I was nothing more than a foot soldier on the losing side of a war I hadn't even realized was being fought.

"Fine, the evolution of the paranormal world from a wicked authoritarian dictatorship to multi-species inept democracy. Better?" Without waiting for an answer, she pushed on. "Many witches in Paranormopolis were thrown out of their homes, places they'd occupied for centuries to make room for other paranormal species."

That was true.

"We can't assume that Cassandra only houses human people who have a knack for communicating with the dead because we don't really know where those witches are now or what they're up to. You don't control them anymore. This is something you should be aware of more than most, my dear." She looked up. "Once upon a time, you were the one in charge of keeping us in line, weren't you?"

Ouch.

"Damn, Astra, your aunt makes you sound like a Nazi," Emma said, her tone level.

"I wasn't a Nazi. Not even close," I snapped defensively.

Emma blinked. "Sorry. Too soon?" She stared at me. "It was too soon, wasn't it. Yeah. Yeah, sorry." The former soldier shifted from one foot to the other, her cheeks pink. "I should have known better. My bad."

WE JUMPED when a horrendous shriek erupted from the outside.

"Watch out! Look out! I'm gonna crash!" Archie screeched. Several thumps, the clanging of metal, and then the loud clinking of broken glass reached us all the way from the backyard. "You stupid idiot! I was trying to help you out! See if I bother with you bird-brained idiots again!"

"Archie?" I raced down the hall, across the living room, and sailed out the back door onto the patio with everyone else in hot pursuit. There, looking pathetic, was the self-proclaimed goddess's own owl, face planted against a chair.

Upside down.

On his head.

"Are you okay? What happened?" Feathers stuck out in wild directions, his chest heaving with deep gasps. "Are you hurt?"

"My pride! My sense of community! My desire to help other birds! Stupid hawk wanted to eat a stupid rabbit, and I tried to tell the idiot he'd have indigestion for a week thanks to Althea and her stupid potions! Did he thank me? Tell me he appreciated the advice? No! Not even close!" The bird's hindquarters slid down the leg of the chair as he continued to complain. "He attacked me. Attacked me! Me! The—"

"Goddess's very own owl," Ayla, Thea, Ami,

and I said in unison as Archie landed on his back with a thump.

Emma looked concerned but confused.

Archie blinked in our direction, then turned away to shake his feathers. When he was done, he turned back and glared at each of us individually with an exaggerated air of indignation. Then, finally, he huffed and scurried into the house, muttering things I shouldn't repeat out loud.

"Anything I should be concerned about?" Emma asked.

"Only if you're the local hawk," Thea told her with a snort.

She frowned. "No information about the fire at all?"

"You look disappointed," I observed as we all moved back into the house.

"Well, yeah, actually." Emma closed the back door and followed my sisters toward the colossal dinner table set for seven. "I think I've started to expect startling revelations from the owl. That, and he didn't come with us today. Even though it was kind of a magic-ish assignment."

"Wasn't *my* assignment. Tell the detective that I only care about star card cases, and this wasn't one of them," Archie said from his perch at the end of the table. "I'm here to help with star card cases, and the rest of the time, I can do what I want when I want."

I did.

"Must be nice," Emma said, pulling out her chair. She sniffed the air. "Wow, that smells great. Some special witchcraft thing cooked in a cauldron?"

"Spaghetti," Aunt Gwennie said as she placed a large bowl at the center of the table. "Cooked in a pot. The garlic bread does have a sprinkling of Thea's herbal concoctions on the top, though. I think the butter's infused, too."

My mother led the table in a prayer of thanks to the goddess Athena. Then everyone grew uncharacteristically quiet as we dug into the carb-loaded meal.

I was halfway through dinner when my mother's eyes found mine.

"Now that we've all eaten a bit." Mom smiled, then her expression grew serious. "I have looked through the books I have and consulted with the oracles about the mystery of the disappearing ghosts," my mother began, her brows arched. "There are very few instances in history or myths of ghosts simply vanishing from a locale. The few times something like that has been mentioned," my mother said, her expression grim, "their disappearance was traced to the ministry."

"What ministry?" Emma asked. "Astra's ministry?"

"Well, she's not talking about the metal band," Thea quipped.

"No way," I told her, shaking my head. "First of all, there *isn't* a ministry anymore. It was disbanded along with my future military career, remember? And second, we didn't have the capability that I know of. We couldn't imprison or move ghosts on this scale, Mom. You know as well as I do—you have to work with them one at a time."

"Well, normally, yes," Aunt Gwennie said, nodding. "But you have a trunk full of devices that theoretically shouldn't have the power they do, Astra. I have no doubt somewhere along the line, the military concocted something that could affect a large area of land. After all, the Witches' Council could shield entire towns. There were the circuses and their bubbles of protection. It's not unheard of."

My mother nodded. "And in the confusion of the last days of the Witches' Council, perhaps someone stole those devices." Mom grabbed her drink, and right before she sipped, she added, "You know, the way you did."

"Hey. I'm not a thief. I was issued that stuff. I just…didn't turn it back in."

"Right, like that makes it okay," Ami said with an eye roll.

"But to what end?" Emma asked, curious. "Why would someone do that? Steal a magical mass destruction weapon."

"That's difficult to say without more information," Mom told her. "And again, we don't know that's what happened. Right now, it's just a hypothesis."

"They did say some pretty weird stuff in that town meeting," I told my mother. I sat back in my chair and slouched. "It seems like the whole town depends on the ghosts to protect it. Like the spirits that haunted the place were a coordinated early warning system that kept crimes from happening or fires from burning." I tapped my finger on the table. "If that's true, the place is utterly defenseless."

"And has been for a month," Emma said.

"And right before they're about to have the largest crowds they'll have all year," Ami pointed out.

"That occurred to me, too." Emma rubbed her

eyes. "But is it really true? I mean, would people really depend on ghosts to stop crimes, stop fires, patrol the town? Are ghosts really that reliable?" She turned to my mother. "I thought they rattled chains and howled at night and maybe made a room a little cold." My mother smiled at Emma. "I mean, I know that's a little simplistic, but these aren't full-fledged beings, are they?"

"Some are, some aren't," Aunt Gwennie answered. "Ayla and Minnie could tell you better than I could, but from what I understand, the ghosts that inhabited Cassandra were all full-fledged beings living the second act of spirit life on this cosmic plane."

Ayla nodded. "I knew someone that had been there for over two hundred years."

"What concerns me most about what you girls said is that Guru Bernie sounds completely unlike himself," my mother said, leaning back in her chair. "I've met the man multiple times, and he's a kindly old man with a warm smile for everyone. He reminds me of that Bernie Sanders, accent and all—if Senator Sanders was a new age religious leader, anyway. The thing that's most concerning?" Mom leaned forward with a concerned expression. "His new cigarette habit."

"Well, not necessarily," Althea said, leaning

forward. "Tobacco has been used for thousands of years by indigenous people for healing. In South America, there are shamans called *tabaqueros* devoted to the ceremonial use of tobacco as a sacred herb. One of the things tobacco was used for? To see ghosts. So there could be some type of arcane explanation."

"Wait. Are you saying all we have to do to talk to the ghosts is smoke a cigarette?" I asked her.

"Don't even think about it," my mother snapped at Ayla when her mouth opened.

"No, that's not what I'm saying." Althea frowned. "Besides, commercial tobacco is *not* sacred. Traditional tobacco is free of chemicals and poisons, so the guru smoking a store-bought cigarette is out of character, anyway. What I'm saying is maybe there is something wrong, and this is the best he can do considering the situation."

"What situation?" Emma asked.

Thea held up her hands in a perplexed gesture.

I looked at Althea. "You think someone's controlling the guru?"

"Maybe, yeah. It's a guess."

"And you came to this based on the fact that

he's smoking cigarettes? That's not just a guess, Thea. That's—"

"Yeah, I know. It seems out of left field. But it popped into my head as soon as Mom said something about him smoking, and she's always saying we should trust those instincts. That sometimes, it's the universe trying to tell us something. I just...I don't know. I felt it."

"She's on to something," Ami said. Then she held up the Judgment card.

"So, I don't mean to poke a stick in everyone's eye," Emma said, her tone hesitating. "But how much can I—as a police investigator—rely on Thea's gut and Ami's deck of cards? I know it seems like I should be used to all this, but I feel like I'm suddenly stuck in an episode of *Supernatural*. It doesn't seem all that reliable to me."

"It's as reliable as the timeline of the universe," my mother answered.

"Yeah, that's not helping. I watched the 'Loki' Marvel show on Disney+," Emma joked, additionally referencing a recent show that presented the timeline as something constantly changing and overwhelmingly in flux.

"You watch an awful lot of television," I observed.

"I'm warning you: don't judge me," she answered back.

"Okay, so everyone makes choices and decisions, right?" Althea said, her hand extending toward Emma. "Well, as soon as you do, the timeline path kind of lines up before you. There's a road and a destination, and you're likely to go from point A to point B if everything continues on its path."

"Unless you get hit by a car," Ayla told the detective.

"Right," Althea nodded. "Something unexpected, something unforeseen—those things can always derail a path. So, divination is only as reliable as the unforeseen possibilities of interference not yet set into motion."

"Beautifully said, niece," Aunt Gwennie said proudly.

Emma stared at Althea. "To simplify, then— it's reliable. Except when it's not."

"Exactly," Thea nodded, smiling.

Emma rolled her eyes.

THE DOORBELL RANG JUST as we finished our dessert—adorable owl-shaped cupcakes in honor of Archie.

"I got it. You guys finish."

I got up and walked down the hall. Through the one-way glass on the front door, I saw Captain Harmon's hulking body and red face standing on the front porch. "Sir," I said after opening it, nodding.

Captain Harmon pushed passed me with barely a hello, and I closed the door behind him. "I saw Emma's car outside. Is she here?" His tone was slightly anxious.

"In the dining room finishing dinner—"

He walked away from me without allowing me to finish my sentence.

As soon as he entered the dining room, the tension vibrated like a live wire. Captain Harmon walked forward immediately, stood over Emma, and glared. "Another home in Cassandra has burned to the ground while you kicked back here at Arden House," he said with a note of asperity in his voice. "I know I didn't give you much to go on—"

"No, sir, you didn't," Emma responded just as brusquely. "You also didn't mention that you were dating the possible arson victim." She wiped her mouth with a napkin, balled it up, and then threw it down on her place. "As much as I normally respect you, Captain—you know damn well that was something you should have disclosed."

"What would that have mattered?" he asked with great hostility.

I didn't know what to do, to be honest. All day Emma seemed like she was in good spirits, jovial and joking. Saying she would tease Captain Harmon about his secret girlfriend once they spoke. She'd hidden her anger at him incredibly well.

Until now, anyway. If he hadn't shown up here unannounced, I doubt I ever would have known how annoyed she was.

"It mattered," she told him flatly. "And I don't even have to answer your question. Because you know it mattered. Sir."

"Captain Harmon, can I get you something to drink?" my mother asked gently. "A cup of coffee, perhaps?"

"No. We have to go. As I said, another house has—"

"Was anyone hurt in the fire?" my mother asked.

A bolt of fear shot through his eyes. "No, but we have to—"

"Captain, please—is anyone in danger currently?"

Captain Harmon stared at my mother, his eyes narrowing as he considered how to handle her. He was obviously annoyed by her interference, but he seemed unsure what he should do about it. Finally, he said, "No, not at the moment."

Ami held up a card toward my mother and nodded.

"Then perhaps we should all sit down in the living room to discuss the situation before running back over to Cassandra," my mother announced as she pulled her chair back from the table. "We all seem to be involved in something we don't quite understand—you included. Perhaps it's time we share information. Sunshine is the best way to dispel the darkness." She paused. "Well, unless you're a vampire, of course."

"Someone's not here," Ami said, holding up the Hermit card. "Someone's not here that should be here."

Emma looked at me. "Call—"

"Oh, no," I told her emphatically. "No way."

"Astra, I'm the least psychic person at this table, and even I know Jason would be the next best thing to having his mother in on this," the detective said. "And we can't bring her here because of their stupid Halloween isolation rules."

"So let's go there," I said, shrugging.

"Astra Arden, I know you know better than that," Aunt Gwennie said with a tsk-tsk. "This is a magical geographical problem. We don't want to go into the geographical area affected to discuss the magical problem. Not before we understand the issue."

My mother nodded sagely. "Call the young man, Astra."

"I promise not to attack him," Archie added. Then he paused. "Mostly."

CHAPTER TEN

*E*veryone congregated in the ritual room. The walls and ceiling were made of white painted plaster, hung with thick, red velvet draperies. The carpet, a deep crimson, showed off the white pattern's exceedingly intricate and exceptionally vivid colors.

It was the only room large enough to comfortably fit us all, once Jason showed up. It also ensured that my mother sat at the center of the circle, clearly and unequivocally leading this informal inquiry.

"Should we wait?" I asked, glancing at my phone. "Jason just texted that he was about ten minutes away."

"Let's just get started." Emma nodded at my

mother and tossed a pillow down on the floor. "We can catch him up or write down any questions we have for him."

"Captain," my mother began with a nod. Her tone of voice was strong and assured. "I think you should start at the beginning. Can you tell us precisely how you got involved with what's going on in Cassandra, and why Emma and Astra were sent to investigate a fire that may have been nothing more than an accident?"

Captain Harmon, annoyed, stood at the far side of the circle opposite Mom. He looked at my mother with a severe expression on his face. "While I appreciate your interest," he said, clenching his teeth, "where I assign my investigators is really none of your concern, Ms. Arden. This is a waste of time."

"Oh, you have got to be kidding me. Enough of this. What the hell has gotten into you, Captain?" Emma burst out, frowning. "None of this is like you. At all."

Emma didn't detail her frustration, but she wasn't mistaken in the little she did say. Harmon was a calm, collected individual who didn't get easily agitated. I couldn't recall ever seeing him furious or shaken by anything he'd witnessed before, no matter how strange it was.

And Emma and I had shown him pretty weird things.

Harmon deflected. "There's a house fire right now—"

"And how did you find out about that house fire, Captain?" my mother asked politely, her expression bland in the face of his verbal parry. "Forkbridge doesn't share jurisdiction with Cassandra. In fact, I believe the municipal ordinances strictly prohibit our resources being used outside of the town's boundaries without a vote of the Advisory Board."

Suddenly, Harmon's expression morphed from impatient to anxious. "How would you even know that?"

"Because I'm on the Forkbridge Advisory Board, Captain. You'd know that if you ever bothered to ask us for anything," my mother's voice thundered across the room as the captain's eyes widened in surprise. "Did you think I would build a home, have a family, open a business, and run the goddess Athena's temple in a town I had no control over?" my mother asked him. "Unless my fellow advisors cut me out of a meeting—and believe me, Captain, they would never do that— you are in breach of the Forkbridge charter and bylaws." She wiggled her toes on the carpeting while Captain Harmon stared at her naked feet. "So, let's start again, shall we?"

Ayla looked impressed. "Wow, Mom doesn't take any—"

"Quiet, Ayla," Aunt Gwennie warned my sister.

As my aunt finished speaking, the rear door was carefully opened, and a casually dressed Jason walked in. "Is this the location of the, uh, meeting?" He inspected the circle of women (and one captain), smiled when he saw me, and walked in without asking permission. "Hello, everyone. I hope you're having a good evening. I'm not sure what kind of assistance I can provide, but I'd be pleased to try."

"No way. I'm not having this conversation with him here," Captain Harmon said quickly, pointing at Jason. "I don't know what his mother's told him or what she wants him to know and not know. I can't talk freely with him listening."

"Captain, you weren't talking freely before he got here," Althea pointed out.

"And you're not planning on being honest with us, anyway," Ami said, holding up the Knight of Swords. "It was reversed. Planning on stabbing us in the back, Captain?"

"Yeah, well, the King of Swords didn't come up, so maybe he's not in charge," Ayla said with a nod. Then her eyes narrowed. "Who's pulling your strings, Captain Grumpypants?"

"Okay, that's enough, all of you." I stood up and pointed to my floor pillow, waving to Jason. He nodded and took a seat. "You, too, Mom. How about we start the ball rolling? So far, there are a few things we know about Captain Harmon— one, he asked Emma to work on a case we weren't really prepared for, and that was out of our jurisdiction. Two? That he's involved with the first possible arson victim, who also happens to be the mayor of Cassandra. And three, that he's not acting like himself." I looked at the Captain. "None of those things scream evil double-agent." I paused. "They do indicate he's afraid of something."

Emma frowned.

"Afraid of something?" Ami asked, dropping her head and shuffling her cards. "Why would you say that?"

"Nothing he's done has been in secret," I pointed out. "He's not trying to hide his activity. He knows he broke the Advisory code or whatever to send us over there. I mean, the whole station knows we were sent over to Cassandra.

So if what you say is true, Mom, that means he's risking his job. He doesn't care." I looked him directly in the eye. "He's afraid, and he doesn't know what to do."

"The Knight of Wands was reversed, actually," Ami said while shuffling her deck. "That *could* mean frustration. Delays."

Harmon rolled his eyes and gave an irritable sigh. Then he muttered something under his breath. "Whatever I'm risking, right now, I am still the captain. Not that anyone would know it from the fact that I'm stuck in a bad episode of *Buffy the Vampire Slayer*."

"Naw, not really," Ayla said with a shrug. "No vampires. This is more like the *X-files*, really. Because you're the government, and we don't trust you."

"Captain, if something is going on, *you* have to tell us," Emma told him, her voice still edged with annoyance. "You told me once that cases like this —ones involving the unexplained—require steadfastness and resilience. Do you remember why you told me that?" I could sense his uncertainty, the question in his eyes as he peered back at her. "Because no one is willing to talk. Because people are more afraid of a curse they can't see than a gun they can see."

This final sentence felt as if it were loaded with meaning that could go in many directions.

Finally, Harmon cleared his throat and then spoke relatively formally. "I love Lil," he said almost apologetically, glancing at Jason. "I do. I planned to ask her to marry me. Now, she doesn't know that, so if you could keep that to yourself, I'd appreciate it." Jason nodded and smiled at the man aspiring to be his step-father. "But ever since I decided to do it? Everything in Cassandra has gone to hell."

I WAS IMPRESSED my mother ceded leading the discussion (if not her place at the head of the circle) long enough for us to make some progress with Captain Harmon.

"Maybe I should have thought more before I went to the jewelry store," Harmon began, his shoulders tight as he sat on the floor. "But I knew Cassandra was important to Lil, and I wanted to get the ring from the official Cassandran jeweler to show her that I respected her beliefs, her—"

"I'm sorry to interrupt so soon after you started, Captain, but did you get the ring at

Aurora Vibrations?" Jason asked, referencing the only fine jewelry shop in Cassandra.

"I did, son; why?"

Immediately, Jason tensed up slightly. "As much as I respect your relationship with my mother, Mr. Harmon, I'd appreciate it if you didn't call me son."

"Of course," Harmon said. "Sorry about that. I meant no offense," he added, sympathetic to Jason's obvious discomfort.

"No offense taken. I'd just prefer not to be called that."

Harmon nodded. "As I said, I was getting the ring from the official Cassandran jeweler, but I decided to buy another trinket for her at Aurora Vibrations. It just hit me, you know? That I should get her something else. I decided to go for a small silver pendant with a small dolomite stone." He smiled. "Lil loves pink. It was a three-dimensional hexagon. It seemed perfect."

My mother frowned. "Hexagons are as close to magic as science gets."

Harmon looked at her. "What do you mean?"

"If you spin a bucket of water fast enough? It turns into a hexagon. Science has never been able to explain why. Well," she smiled. "At least not yet. In California, there's the Devils Postpile—basalt columns left by a lava flow, all hexagonal in shape. Then, of course, there's a bee's honeycomb. What most people aren't aware of?" My mother sighed almost lovingly. "The hexagon is encoded into their very eyes."

Captain Harmon stared at her like she was off her rocker.

Emma cleared her throat. "You know, I knew all that—but somehow, when you say it, it seems super spooky and weird and significant," she told my mother.

Mom smiled. "It is believed that bees use hexagons because the hexagons tessellate." We must have all looked confused. "Hexagons can be repeated again and over again without creating gaps or overlapping. Understand?"

We all nodded, even though I'm sure at least half of us had absolutely no clue what the crazy hippie woman was getting at.

"Consequently, it is the most effective method of packing a space with the least possible quantity of material holding it," my mother told Emma. "Triangles and squares tessellate; circles and pentagons do not. Hexagons, which are themselves composed of tessellated triangles, do."

Uh-huh.

I nodded again.

I still had no idea what the crazy hippie lady was getting at.

"I don't see what this has to do with the necklace I bought," Harmon pointed out.

I was glad he said it.

"Bees don't create hexagons," my mother told him.

"But you just said—"

"I know what I said," she smiled at him. "Honeycomb cells start off as circles within the first few seconds of formation and then eventually morph into hexagons. Once the wax starts flowing, the cell walls naturally fall flat and take on a hexagon shape. You understand? Like adjoining bubbles in a bath."

"Look, Ms. Arden, I hear you," Harmon responded, agitated. "I still don't understand your point."

"The circle turns into a hexagon once something is *in* the honeycomb, Captain Harmon," my mother told him—as if that explained everything. Which it didn't. "Let me guess. You purchased this necklace about a month ago?"

Captain Harmon blinked, and Jason gasped. Emma's head jerked back as the pieces fell into place. "Wait a minute, wait a minute. Are you saying you think the mayor is wearing the ghosts around her neck?" Emma asked my mother.

"That's not possible," Captain Harmon said, shaking his head.

"Right, because *you* would know about possible and impossible?" Ayla said and then snorted with an eye roll. "Humans."

"Ayla." Aunt Gwennie's glare was no joke.

"Dolomite helps to connect someone to the spirit world," my mother explained, her hands clasped in front of her. "It's also a powerful channel, allowing someone that works with it the ability to tap into the vast, unlimited power of nature. Dolomite's earth element paired with a powerful grounding stone can result in an almost unstoppable energy force." Mom glanced around, meeting each of our eyes. "A magical user could certainly craft a hexagon stone that worked, effectively, as a spirit prison or prison key."

Only Aunt Gwennie didn't look surprised by Mom's conclusion.

"Look, I hate to ruin a good story, but I don't know about any of that," Captain Harmon said, waving his hand toward my mother as if in dismissal. "And I don't think you understand me. The problems in Cassandra didn't start when I bought the necklace. The problems started when Lil *lost* it the day after I gave it to her."

"What problems started?" Emma asked. Even though I could see from her expression, she already knew the answer.

"That's when the ghosts disappeared."

"Do you buy that?" Emma asked me quietly.

The two of us were standing to the side of the ritual room alone. Ami and Ayla were flipping through a book on crystals so they would have a good idea of what the necklace looked like. Captain Harmon was enduring a brutal lecture from my mother on not telling us the full story at the outset of the case (and before sending her daughters into Cassandra).

"Buy what? His story or hers?" I asked, pointing to the pair.

"Take your pick," she said. Crossing her arms, she eyed the two. "I've met pixies. My brother's a vampire. I get it. Unexplained things and all that. I can roll with the punches, Arden, I really can." She pointed. "But you guys seem to get the smallest nugget of information and wind up spinning a yarn that defies explanation. Or no, not defies it—explains everything with no proof of anything."

"Welcome to Arden Coven."

"Har har. I'm serious."

"Okay, so, you're not quite right. It doesn't explain everything," I told her, turning my back on the room and lowering my voice. "We didn't mention anything in that circle about the mayor's house or why it was set on fire. Everyone was so busy yapping their mouths and explaining how a beehive functions that we still don't even know what other place got set on fire."

"Yeah, that's true," Emma admitted, gazing out at the room.

"Excuse me, Astra? Emma?" I turned around to find Jason about five feet away. "Can I talk to you both for a moment?"

"Sure." Emma waved him over. "What's up, handsome?"

Jason smiled faintly as he joined us. "I didn't want to say anything in front of the captain, but I did want to mention to the two of you. Aurora Vibrations? It's owned by Robert and Jane Aurora. They're new in town, and I don't know much about them, actually."

"How new?" Emma asked him.

"Six months, maybe?"

Six months?

That's how long I'd been back in Forkbridge.

Come to think of it, that's about how long it's been since Paranormopolis emptied out of witches. At least, witches that sided with the Witches' Council.

"You guys take new members into your religious sect thing?" I asked, surprised. "I thought only members of your...um...church could live within the bounds of the town proper since it's all private property."

Yes, I was going to say cult.

I stopped myself.

"Rarely, but yes, we do," Jason answered. "You actually met Robert. He was a member of the fire tenders? The one that told you my mother wanted to restrict gas-powered cars within the town limits?"

Right.

He did not want to say his last name. I recalled Robert also told me the elders cut off communication with the ghosts and turned the spirit world into Cassandra's private spirit library for elite psychics.

Which, I reminded myself, was something we hadn't confirmed with anyone else—and a claim entirely against what Serena Bliss told the rest of the Cassandrans at the town hall meeting.

"You want to share with the class what the gerbils in your head are talking about while they run on that wheel?" Emma asked, catching my expression.

"In a sec. If Robert owns a business, what was he doing there in the fire house?" I asked Jason.

He shrugged. "Like I said, I don't know much about him. I just know he's new, and he and his wife showed up one day out of the blue." Jason leaned forward. "To tell you the truth, my mother didn't seem all that happy they were accepted."

Emma raised an eyebrow. "Wouldn't she be the one accepting them?"

He shook his head. "The guru handles the religious stuff. She handles the bureaucratic town stuff. And Serena handles whatever the two of them need her to handle, I guess."

I nodded. "Quick question—the mayor is elected, right?"

Jason nodded.

"What's the term?"

"All three of the terms are for life." Emma and I looked at each other in a speechless conclave. "The mayor, the guru, and the assistant. Once chosen, they serve until they choose to step down, or they die." Jason caught our expressions. "What?"

"You guys don't have any mechanism for, like, a recall election?" Emma asked, surprised.

"Nope. It's a different kind of place, you know."

Emma laughed sharply. "Oh, believe me, if we didn't know before? We sure do now."

CHAPTER ELEVEN

*B*ecause it was late, Mom insisted that we leave Ayla at home.

Ayla was...displeased.

At first look, the tiny hamlet known for psychics resembled a paranormal version of Colonial Williamsburg, a psychic/hippie counterpart to the living-history museum. People traveled there for the readings, but they stayed for the new age expo on the streets, in the shops, and in restaurants.

There have always been places around the world where, intentionally or accidentally, communities have grown up to include many people with paranormal beliefs. I doubted any, though, could compete with Cassandra in terms of dedication to the spiritual ideal in every square inch of the town.

Case in point?

A house fire as the evening's entertainment.

"That's Madame Margo's house," Emma murmured, her face bathed in bright orange from the fire. "She's one of the top psychics in town."

I looked at Emma.

She stared back. "Madame Margo Morgan?"

"Never heard of her. Surprised you have," I said dryly.

"What? I've gotten psychic readings."

Madame Margo Morgan's split-level home just off the main strip was burning in a conflagration of melting plastic flowers, potted palms, and cracking glass wind chimes. The fire men raced around swiftly, surrounding the burning home with stacked cinder blocks as if forming a containment perimeter. Crowds of tourists gathered to watch them work, smiling and laughing, red solo cups of some liquid in their hands.

There was something deeply unsettling about the scene.

"This is wild!" a blond girl in a caftan shrieked, her eyes wide with excitement. "They've really gone all out this year for Halloween!

Nathan!" She turned and thrust her cup at a man standing behind her. "Get me more Holy Spirits. The berry-flavored."

"What's going to happen to Madame Margo's schedule?" another woman asked. "I came all the way from Maine for my reading! She'll still be doing the readings even though her house burned down, right?"

The fire man passing by glared at the woman and continued laying out barriers.

"Well, she's not IN there, is she?" the woman called. "You! You there! Madame Margo isn't dead, is she? I pre-paid for my reading, and it was a lot!"

Temporary wooden planks were erected just past the cinderblocks. They acted as a barrier to hold the crowd back—but I couldn't tell if they were protecting the public from the fire or the fire from the crowd.

"These people are something else, let me tell you," Emma commented.

"I don't get it," I told her quietly. "Why aren't they putting the fire out? The captain told us about this more than an hour ago."

When we arrived, it was immediately apparent how bad things were. I knew nothing about fire—save it could be hot—but I could see

184 | LEANNE LEEDS

this blaze intended to eat the entire structure quickly. "There are at least a hundred people here watching this like it's some kind of show."

"It *is* some kind of show, Ms. Arden," the mayor said as she joined Emma and me. The captain stood by her side protectively. "The fire tenders have determined that Madame Margo's home wanted to burn, that the fire intended to be here." She looked troubled. "Since they decided that, we will all stand here until it burns to the ground."

The night wind whipped the scorching flames around gently, sparks flying. As a second floor room collapsed in a roar, the crowd cheered.

"This is crazy," I muttered.

The captain caught my eye, a mournful expression on his face. He sighed, put his arm around the mayor's shoulders, and said, "I respect your right to believe what you want, Lil—you know I do. But Astra's right. This just seems crazy to me."

The mayor's face looked pained. "I know how it looks, Daniel. There are some parts of all this I sometimes think may have gotten out of hand." She looked around at the crowd of visitors laughing, drinking, and gawking at the spectacle of a house being incinerated. "But no one's been hurt. Margo will have a place to sleep tonight. The community will take care of her."

"Well, at least we know you aren't the person being targeted now," Emma pointed out. "Unless Margo is related to you somehow? Some tie I don't know about?"

"No, she's not," the mayor said. "Related to me, I mean. I know her, of course. I'm the most in-demand psychic in Cassandra, but she's the second most in-demand. So my assistant works with hers on appointments, especially if someone's already planning on coming and I can't fit them in."

The mayor's expression was drawn and worn. Her eyeshadow was smudged, and she had black bags under her eyes. The fires, Halloween, and the mystery of who was burning down homes in Cassandra—and why—were clearly taking a toll on her.

"Where are Madame Margot and her assistant?" I asked, looking around. "I'd like to get a look at them before we have to talk to them."

"Margot and Jinny are over there," Jason, who'd been silently listening this whole time, told me. He pointed toward a small area off the side of the burning house. "The two of them are talking to Robert Aurora."

"Robert, the guy that owns Aurora Vibrations?" I asked, my Spidey-sense crackling cold even as the heat of the burning building warmed me. I leaned my head back and stretched my neck to get a better view. "That Robert?"

"Yes."

Robert Aurora was Robert the fire tender. Also known as Robert, the guy that wouldn't tell me his last name when we visited the fire house. He was also Robert, the guy who told me ghosts have to be checked out of a psychic library like books. Oh, and Robert the only-been-here-six-months dude.

I looked back at the house and sniffed the air.

Gasoline.

Robert's eyes narrowed, flames shining in his eyes, as the burning wood cracked and collapsed.

IT TOOK the fire another hour to completely burn down the house. It would have gone up much faster had it been newer and had fewer bricks, but it was an older home and extremely well-built. I stepped toward it after the flames died down and the charred ruins had settled into a smoking, flat wreck.

"That's still hot," Jason cautioned.

"My outfit and boots are fireproof," I told him over my shoulder, nodding.

"If anything looks suspicious or dangerous, you come right out of there," Emma warned me. "My boots aren't fireproof, and they're expensive as hell, Arden. I don't want to have to replace them because they melted when I ran in after you."

The stench of gasoline was strong in the air.

I stood up straight and looked around from the center of the wreckage. The fire had destroyed the home thoroughly, but nothing else. No trees went up, no cars were damaged. The house to the right stood tall and unscathed. On the left, the Piggy Pickle Shack BBQ Joint didn't have so much as a smudge of ash. "There's no way a fire could burn this neatly without real firemen to contain it," I muttered to myself. "Nothing outside the property line is burned. The heat didn't even melt it."

"God protected the rest of the town, of course," a raspy voice called out. I turned and came face to face with a bare-chested Guru Bernie sporting dhoti (loose pants more commonly seen in India). The old man's eyes twinkled with malice as he walked, barefoot, over the hot coals. The crowd gasped with delight and applauded again. "Why else would only this parcel burn?"

The guru's voice was deeper than it had been when I first saw him, and there was no trace of the heavy Brooklyn accent my mother claimed Bernie possessed. Then, just as I was about to speak, my eyes dropped to the guru's chest.

A pendant made of pink stone.

In the shape of a hexagon.

Is it possible that my mother was correct?

Is this man wearing a prison of ghosts around his neck?

I ticked through several ways to play this and settled on genuflection.

"Guru Bernie," I murmured, bowing politely and clasping my hands. I pretended to be deferential to the suspicious religious leader as we stood in the middle of the glowing rubble like we were on stage. I grinned brightly as I stood up. "It's an honor to firewalk with you. Truly." My gaze flitted back and forth. "It's amazing that you've let these people witness something so sacred."

The guru and I were sure to be the subject of many woke Instagram posts by the following day as cell phone flashes pierced the darkness.

"That's why I'm here," Bernie responded loud and clear so everyone gathered could hear. "However, Astra, I have a question for you. What are you doing here?" He took a pack of Marlboro Reds from his loose-fitting trousers pocket. Bernie inhaled deeply after lighting the cigarette. "You had a meeting with the fire tenders. You know. What's going on here is supposed to happen."

Another drag.

I smiled.

He lowered his voice and stepped closer. In a voice only I could hear, he hissed, "Go home, witch."

I smiled wider and didn't respond.

The guru appeared to ready a mouthful of smoke to blow directly into my face, but then he looked around at the audience and decided against it.

"Of course, Guru Bernie," I gushed, bowing again. "Anything you say, Guru Bernie. This is, after all, your domain."

The old man's eyes narrowed.

After one more exaggerated bow, I turned and headed back toward Emma, grabbed her arm, and walked her away from the fire. "Keep walking," I said in hushed tones. The captain and the mayor, who appeared to be taken aback, hastened to catch up with us.

"What was that all about?" Emma asked once we'd cleared the watch-the-world-burn crowd.

"There must be a video of that guy talking to his followers somewhere, right?" I asked her, but she only shrugged. I turned toward Jason. "Somewhere we can find video of what he normally sounds like? Can you think of any place? Quick."

He pointed toward a building on the next block. "The visitor's center? Joe Gillespie should be there since it's Halloween. They stay open until midnight during the festival, maybe even after with this many people."

Emma grabbed my arm. "Astra, what's going on?"

"I want to see a video first. Then I'll explain."

JOE GILLESPIE WAS in his sixties and had wispy hair on the top of his head. He led us to the back room, where a wall of VHS cassettes lined the rear wall. "I wish we had something a little more modern, but you're welcome to look at any of the guru's sermon tapes." Before leaving the room, he pointed to a large VHS player connected to a television that was probably out of date in the 1990s.

I reviewed the tapes' dates and pulled a three-month-old lecture and a three-week-old lecture. I inserted the first.

"What exactly are we looking for?" Emma inquired as the group sat in chairs around a wide library-style table. "Is there anything in particular?"

"I just want to hear how he sounds before saying anything." I inserted the first tape, which was three months old, and clicked the play button. The screen filled with snow, then with squiggled lines, and eventually with a clear picture.

"We are blessed to be able to give people a pathway into the ever after," Guru Bernie said with a heavy New York accent. "Blessed that people know to come to us, yes? Blessed that we all found each other and that we get to live among people that want to do good for other people, yes? Yes?" He chuckled endearingly. "Of course, yes. Who would say no to that?"

This guy sounded nothing like the man I just met.

At all.

The old man's eyes danced with amusement as he encouraged his followers to celebrate themselves. "Sure, we get the rich people wanting to know where the lost insurance policy is, or the deep-pocketed folks that want to come just to make sure someone they didn't like is miserable in the afterlife—"

"Wow, people do that?" Emma asked Lillian Thornton.

"You'd be surprised," said the mayor, nodding. "We attempt to screen them out before they arrive, the ones we probably won't be able to help, but it's difficult. But, you see, we believe we have these skills because they should be available to everyone. Everyone should have access to the limitless beyond. So we get some real prizes." She lowered her gaze to her fumbling hands. "I know, I sound ridiculous considering what you've seen. Like I'm one to talk. But I promise this town isn't as insane as you think it is, Detective Sullivan."

"I don't judge," Emma said hastily, catching my glance.

She did judge. Just sayin'.

I leaned forward and squinted. The guru wore a loose shirt. Due to that, I couldn't be entirely sure he wasn't wearing the pendant I just spotted around his neck. Still, after about ten minutes, I was reasonably sure it wasn't there.

I pushed the eject button and slipped in the tape from three weeks ago. Once I hit play, I turned around to walk back to the table and sit with the others.

"What are you hoping to spot?" Emma asked.

Jason lifted his eyebrows in a silent question.

"I told you. I want to hear how he—"

"This town has been ignored for too long!" an angry voice snarled from behind me. It was so angry and so loud and so different that I jumped. "We have ignored our calling! We have ignored the need for our power!" I turned and stared at the screen as the guru's stormy expression punctuated his thundering words. "The world needs us to lead them! Only we have a connection to God's next level!"

"Wow. That's not arrogant at all," Emma murmured, stunned. "What happened to him?" She turned and looked at the mayor. "What changed?"

"The guru did, I suppose. About a month ago," she told me uncomfortably. Her eyes cast toward Captain Harmon, and he clasped her hand. "Guru Bernie has ultimate authority over our spiritual beliefs, and I've always believed the guru was wise. He has always been wise," she told Emma, her voice dropping.

I hit pause on the VHS. "He probably is still wise."

She looked up, her eyes pained. "What do you mean?"

"Do you see that?" I asked, pointing to the faint pink stone resting on the guru's bare chest. "That necklace?"

"No way," Emma breathed, scrambling out of her chair toward the television. Jason followed her. "Are you telling me your mother was right?"

"Your mother?" Lillian Thornton asked. "The high priestess?"

"We met with Astra's coven before coming over here," Harmon told her. "Mrs. Arden has a theory about beehives and hexadecimals—"

"Hexagons," I corrected him.

"—that I didn't quite understand, to be honest with you." He squeezed Lil's hand. "You thought the guru was angry with you because he blamed you for the ghosts disappearing, and that's why he's been acting so crazy the last month. That the loss of the ghosts drove him a little whackadoo." Captain Harmon glanced at me. "The witches have a different idea."

The mayor looked at him. "I don't understand."

"Mayor, do you recognize that necklace?" I asked, waving toward the screen.

Reluctantly releasing Captain Harmon's hand, Lillian Thornton got up and walked toward the screen. Jason and Emma stepped out of her way so she could lean closer. She squinted. "That's…" Her eyes widened. "Is that the necklace you gave me, Daniel?" She looked back at him. "Come look at this. I could swear this is the pendant I lost."

"I don't have to," he said flatly. "I'm pretty sure it is."

Lil stood up. "I don't understand. What are you all telling me?"

Jason stepped toward his mother. "Mom, have you been able to talk to any ghosts since you lost that pendant?"

"No, no one has, Jason," she told him with a toss of her head. "Well, none of the psychics. Only the guru's been able to communicate with the great beyond. That's why he's been so out of sorts lately. He's been doing all the readings himself."

I raised my hand. "I thought you guys check the ghosts out? Like a library?"

Lilian Thornton stared at me like I was brain dead. "Who on earth told you that?"

Emma and I looked at one another. "Well, damn. I just became the sidekick, didn't I? This is some crazy magic conspiracy."

I smiled and shrugged. "Sorry?"

My phone buzzed. I tapped it and opened my texts.

It was from Ami.

ARCHIE ON THE WAY

It had an image attached.

A glowing star card.

CHAPTER TWELVE

$\mathcal{A}$s the wind blew through the dry leaves in the trees, I thought I heard an owl hoot. My eyes swept the skies for Archie, but he was either taking his time or trying to stay concealed.

"Mayor, I *told* you it was coming," Madame Margo said to Lillian Thornton as three of us— Emma, the mayor, and me—rushed up to her. She was a small woman with dark hair pulled back from her face tightly. Her eyes were a strange gray-green color, similar to the sea on a cloudy day, and she spoke with an unmistakable air of command. "I tried to warn you, and you ignored me." She paused for emphasis. "And it has now happened." Madame Margo crossed her arms and thrust her face out in a dramatic gesture toward the mayor. "My house has been completely destroyed. By *fire*."

Thanks for pointing that out.

We never would have picked up on that.

Before the mayor could respond, Madame Margo's assistant, Jinny, spoke up and added, "Yes, but it wanted to. Burn down to the ground. So it's not all that bad, is it? It was fated to happen. If you look at it in a certain light, you were sort of chosen. Right?" Delicate eyelashes fluttered. "I mean, it must be clearing the way for something new."

Madame Margo gave Jinny a cold stare.

"I'm just saying," the young woman laughed at the older one. Her laughter was shrill and soprano, like a tiny sea lion.

Judging by her demeanor, Madame Margo couldn't care less about her previous home's possible free will decision to burn down or what the smoldering emptiness was making room for.

I looked around at the heap of ashes on the ground. If you didn't know what had been there previously, it would be impossible to discern if the property ever had a house on it. "Did the fire start here?" I asked, pointing to a particularly dark corner.

Margo snapped, "I don't know. How could I possibly know?" The woman responded with a soaring rattle of humorless laughter, but her eyes were enraged.

"Did you hear or see anything before you noticed the fire, Madame Margo?" Emma inquired. Her words were deliberate and slow, and she spoke with a low, hushed tone. My partner had some sharp edges to her but when needed, she could be gentle.

She just didn't think she needed it much.

Margo shook her head. "No, nothing. But then again, I wasn't expecting this."

Emma nodded grimly. "It's okay."

Lillian fixed her gaze on Margo. "You literally just said you thought something terrible would happen. Just stood there and bit my head off for not listening to you because you knew it was coming."

"And now it has!" she cried out. Her eyes again had a wild and feral look, like she was an untamed animal that'd been cornered and was ready to attack.

I looked out at the crowd again.

The faces of people who would never see one another again passed close as they moved around examining the smoldering ruins. The tourists laughed and talked about the amazing thing they'd seen—oblivious to the fact that Margo had just lost everything. Or maybe they weren't oblivious.

Maybe they just didn't care.

A few drunken college students jumped over the barrier with sticks, trying to poke at the embers. They stopped when the fire men called them out, looking guilty.

"I think we should go," I suggested to Madame Margo.

I didn't want to continue this conversation in front of the drunken crowd watching the destruction for entertainment. Sure, they appeared harmless and dumb, but anyone could be hidden among the group of inebriated knuckleheads.

Margo nodded, and I grabbed her arm.

We walked away from the devastation, back toward the visitor center. It was the only place in the town that seemed empty—likely because Joe Gillespie ran the only place in the entire town that didn't serve alcohol.

Suddenly, Margo stopped and turned back to yell at Lillian Thornton. "You can't trust those fire men, you know. They don't care about anyone but themselves."

"I'm sure they do their best," the mayor responded quickly, her face sagging with lines of tension.

"All of them are liars!" Margo yelled. "Every single one of them." She looked around quickly, as if concerned that someone had overheard her. Her face was flushed, her eyes were wide, and her hands were trembling. She appeared to be close to tears. "Ugh." She wiped her brow. "I'm not going to let those jerks see me cry. I'm not going to do it."

"No one would judge you, Madame Margo. You've been through a lot today," I told her.

"Yes," she said. "And it's not over yet. Destruction is simple. Rebuilding? That is always the most difficult part. And I'm getting old, Astra. It's too late to start over." Margo frowned as she looked at the fire men keeping an eye on the crowd. "If I'm even permitted to."

I almost asked what that meant but decided against it.

I didn't want to start the conversation on the street because I wanted to give Madame Margo some time to process what she'd just been through—and get her somewhere she couldn't be overheard.

Because what I wanted to know was this:

what the heck was with this pseudo-firemen group? These idiots couldn't put out a fire, so what the heck was their purpose, anyway? Considering what Madame Margo shouted back at the mayor, she might tell me.

Madame Margo remained silent, and we continued walking down the street, zigzagging our way through the costumed tourists. The wind picked up, blowing the ashes around us. We passed by the fire tenders, who were still working, and they waved at us as we went past.

We made it to the visitors' center without saying anything to each other.

Once inside, I removed my shoes to avoid tracking ash on the floor, and Emma did the same. Madame Margo didn't bother. Instead, she dragged herself across the room, then sat heavily in one of two chairs facing the storefront.

She buried her face in her hands and sobbed.

JOE GILLESPIE GREETED US, clearly pleased to be of service once more. He raced around so speedily that he knocked the noticeboard off the wall. "You can stay as long as you want," he said with a friendly wave. Nodding, he passed Jason a cup of coffee. "It's great to see you back in town for Halloween, Jason. I'm sure your mother is excited to have you."

"Thank you, Joe." Jason managed to crack a slight smile.

"Do you know where the owl is?" Emma wondered out loud.

"He should have turned up by now." I took out my phone and messaged Ami, wanting to know where Archie was. My phone buzzed once she answered with the shrugged shoulder emoji. I pointed my screen at Emma.

"What owl?" Jason asked.

Emma sighed and waved away his question. She appeared tired—and concerned. I followed her gaze to Lillian Thornton standing near the front door, arguing with Jinny, Margo's assistant.

"It's not about the ghosts! Robert told me that the fire ghosts want to give people new places, that's all. They want new people, too. Fire clears things out of the way. He told me!" Jinny fumed with a perky jump up and down. "The fires aren't a bad thing. You just don't know how to change with the times—"

"He did, did he?" the mayor snapped. "He told

you the destruction of our homes, all our possessions, all our worldly goods was a good thing? If your brain was dynamite, young lady, there wouldn't be enough in there to blow a strand of hair from your ponytail!"

"Hey, Miss High and Mighty, what are you yelling at her for?" Madame Margo heaved herself out of her chair, pointing a critical finger at the mayor. "You were the one full of self-pity because Guru gave you a dress-down! And then you hid under a rock while the fire guys ran rampant and took this place over!"

Lillian's brow furrowed in rage. "I did nothing of the sort—"

"Oh, can it, your majesty! You bowed and scraped and took responsibility for something you don't even think you did. Something that poses a threat to this town." Margo glanced at me. "And then you run to the witches of Forkbridge to have them figure it out for you." Madame Margo shifted her gaze back to the mayor. "Don't you get tired of putting makeup on both of your faces every morning?"

Captain Harmon appeared mystified. "Both of her faces?"

"She's calling your girlfriend two-faced, Cap," Emma informed him.

Joe Gillespie stared at the two most famous city soothsayers as they faced off across the room from one another, two cups of coffee gripped in his hands. He appeared to be frozen as if witnessing a reprehensible event. "I brought two more coffees," he said quietly.

"I'll take one of those, please." I took a cup from him.

Emma kept an eye on me. "You've gone strangely quiet all of a sudden."

I sipped the coffee. "Not strange at all. I've always found you can find out a lot of information by staying quiet and listening to people yell at each other. For example: have you noticed that the assistants of the two most powerful psychics in town are strangely defensive of certain suspicious parties?"

That stopped both the mayor and Madame Margo. They turned toward me.

"I had noticed that, Astra. After all, I *am* a detective," Emma said confidently.

"Did you, really?"

The expression on Emma's face told me she really hadn't.

"For those of us that are not skilled in investigative techniques, could you explain what you mean?" Jason asked.

"Something is going on with the guru." I set down my coffee and stepped forward. "Serena Bliss, the mayor's assistant, seems particularly loyal to the guru while being overtly hostile to the mayor. Yet her job is to be an assistant to both of them, not just him." I turned toward Joe, the visitor's center host. "Am I right?"

The man appeared nervous as he was summoned to offer his thoughts amid this squabble. "Well, I'm not sure who's mad at who," he scratched his chin, "but you're right. Serena is both of their assistants. Yeah, that's true. They have a kind of administrative bridge between them."

Lillian Thornton cast a glance at Jinny.

"Now we've had another house catch fire and another assistant that appears to believe this was a good thing." I turned my attention to Jinny. "As noted previously, this place is pretty strange, and you all have some admittedly weird traditions— but you've also been here for over a century. I don't recall any houses being burned down in the past—even though this is being held up as some religious blessing." I relocated my eyes to Joe. "Again—am I wrong?"

"Well, we've had a few fires, to be sure. But not in this way."

I nodded slowly, watching everyone's expressions. "There are no records of these types of events anywhere else. No newspaper articles or anything like that. My sisters looked. In all the years Cassandra has been here, having your house burn to the ground has never been a psychic rite of passage." I glanced around the room. "So, it stands to reason that it's not, and something has changed."

"Our beliefs have changed!" Jinny said hotly.

"No, honey, your guru has changed," I corrected her. "And you all are so devoted to the kindly old guy that's lead you for years that none of you have stopped to notice he's not that kindly old guy right now. All of the ghosts that could have warned you something was off with him have up and disappeared."

And the two assistants were too stupid to notice they were being manipulated.

Or they were in on it.

I hadn't ruled that out yet.

I didn't want to shake these people's beliefs, but the guru who was supposed to protect and guide them wasn't the same zen master he'd been. That no one had noticed the difference, that the congregation had tacitly accepted Bernie's massive shift from a lovable old man to

Sauron without a second thought? That meant someone was pushing an explanation everyone bought.

Who was that, why were they doing it, and what did it have to do with ghosts disappearing? Unfortunately, that wasn't something I had figured out yet.

I had noticed one thing.

Robert's name kept coming up an awful lot.

And his shop sold the mysterious necklace.

"So you think the ghosts disappearing, and Bernie's odd mood have something to do with one another?" Madame Margo asked, her smug look cast at the mayor as she asked.

"Yes, I do."

"Well, I'll be," Margo muttered. "Shame no one else thought of that until now. Oh, wait!" Margo crossed her arms.

The mayor glared back.

ARCHIE LANDED on the ledge just outside the storefront window. He hopped down from his perch and stood in front of the door, tapping his beak against the glass to get our attention.

Emma dashed to the front door and yanked it

open. "Finally! Where have you been? Since you can fly, I would have thought you'd be here—"

Archie blinked. "Do I answer to you?"

Emma stopped and blinked. "I am just glad to—"

The owl tilted his head. "I don't answer to you."

Emma looked at me. "Well, he's in a charming mood."

I raised my eyebrow. "You can understand him?"

The detective nodded. "I guess that I can every time there's a star card case now." The last case, we'd magicked up a way for Emma to understand Archie so she could help with Athena's star card cases. Now that we had one, that power seemed to have kicked back in.

"I have something for you," Archie said as if it were an afterthought, his talons clicking on the floor as he limped in. He held one foot out to me, clutching what appeared to be a small object between two fingers. It was about three inches long and half an inch thick, about the size of my thumb.

Wait.

Are they called fingers?

Toes?

"Your sister slipped it to me just as I was leaving." Archie looked at me with an unspoken accusation, as if I had broken some fundamental trust.

"Which sister?" Emma asked.

"The small, annoying one that Astra's mother thought was upstairs asleep in bed. She was not upstairs in her bed; she was sitting in Astra's room crying because she was left behind by you people." Archie held it out toward me. "You planning on grabbing this thing, or do I have to walk like a pirate the rest of the night and carry it for you?"

"What's gotten into you?" I leaned forward, but Jason jumped forward grabbed my arm. "Ow." I looked at him. "What's wrong?"

His eyes were wide, and he looked agitated. "Astra, what are you doing?" Jason's gaze darted back and forth—toward Archie on the ground, toward the door, toward Emma— then rested on me again. "That's a wild animal. In fact, I think that's the *same* wild animal that attacked me at the park."

Oh. Right.

That.

"An owl attacked you at a park?" Lillian gasped, her mouth open.

"Yeah, but he was fine. That's not a wild animal. That's Astra's paranormal familiar thing," Emma responded without bothering to consult me. She slapped her hand over her mouth within seconds, and her eyes found mine. "Crap. Was I supposed to tell them who Archie is?" I glared back at her. "I mean, I just thought it would be no big deal since they know you're a witch and all."

"Wait a minute, wait a minute. That's *your* pet owl?" Jason asked, incredulous.

"It is not a pet owl because it's illegal to have a pet owl," I responded without enthusiasm. "But Emma's right. It's not a regular owl from the woods. It's"—I paused and thought about how much to say regarding the supposed divine origins of Archimedes the owl—"a paranormal owl. Kind of like a familiar. It helps me on certain investigations."

"It is also not *it*, toots," Archie grumbled, then blinked with exaggerated impatience. "I'm a he, thank you very much. And, by the way, no one has taken this thing yet. I'm getting tired of holding it. I know they can't understand a word I'm saying, but I don't know what excuse either of *you* have."

Emma jumped forward and grabbed the small object. "What is it?"

"It's a stone Ayla says you'll need if any ghosts attack you," Archie explained. He jumped off the ground and flapped his massive wings once to perch on the back of a chair. "She managed to talk to one of her own ghost friends, one that never comes here. All specters, by the way, are avoiding this area like there's a *Ghostbusters* team running around."

We had no idea (though we should have) that the conversation we were having with Archie appeared so threatening to the rest of the people in the room.

Lillian and Jason stood next to the captain with expressions of shock.

Captain Harmon remained alert, his hand on his sidearm.

All three stared at the owl, their faces pale beneath their unhealthy Florida tans.

On the other side of the room, Jinny forcefully averted her gaze like Archie potentially possessed the stone-gazing power of Medusa. She remained seated next to Joe, clutching his arm as if drowning.

Joe's gaze, however, was fixed on Archie's face. He looked awestruck.

"Why would ghosts attack us?" I asked the owl.

"Well, because you're around him," Archie pointed at Jason.

Emma raised her eyebrow. "And why would any ghosts attack him?"

"Because Ami says it's his life in danger, and Athena doesn't want him dead."

CHAPTER THIRTEEN

"What? What are you talking about?" Emma furrowed her brow in response to Archie's reaction. "Jason is the star card? Well, I don't mean he *is* the star card, but... oh, you know what I mean."

"I don't understand. What exactly is the star card?" Lillian inquired.

Everyone in the room cast uneasy glances around—as if something else would happen. Archie narrowed his eyes and cocked his head to the side. "Would you like to inform her?" the owl asked. "I'd tell her, but she has no idea what I'm saying."

I didn't want to tell anyone yet.

"What are you on about, Emma?" Jason's right

eyebrow shot up, and he went immediately toward the front door. Then, glancing out onto the street through the glass, he said, "Ghosts don't attack people, so this is ridiculous. I really think you guys need to start explaining what's going on." He turned and looked at Emma. "You've clearly been hiding something from the rest of us, and now you're threatening my life."

I rolled my eyes. "Jason, she's not threatening your life."

She looked at him with disbelief. "Of course I'm not! And we're not hiding anything. Well, not about what's going on here in Cassandra. That's not what this is about," Emma said, reaching out toward him.

He stepped back with a quick, sharp motion. "Don't touch me."

Everyone froze at the tone in Jason's voice.

Everyone except Archie.

"You know, I was worried when his card flipped over that I was going to have to attack him again," the owl said, leaping onto the table and clicking his claws against the wood. "You both took care of any worries I had with a few sentences. Well done." The owl looked Jason up and down before turning to face Emma and me. "You two need to work on your reveals a lot more. You'd get tomatoes thrown at your head if you were stage magicians."

"Is that owl talking to you?" Jason asked, pointing toward the table with one hand while blocking his mother from Archie's line of sight with his other one.

Emma glanced at me nervously. "He is, but—"

"But what?" Jason turned back toward me, his expression grim. "Astra, what is going on? I've been nothing but honest with you since we've met. None of what's going on here is an accident, and I'd like to be able to trust you, at least. But I don't understand what's happening here."

The guilt I felt about not taking the mayor's house fire seriously came rushing back in the face of Jason's concerned expression. "You're right. You have been honest with me any time I've asked, and you've been willing to traipse along behind us and explain the weirdness in this town, so I'll level with you." I looked around. "All of you."

I gave those in the room a brief history of my job in the paranormal military, an account of the revolution and new government, and my termination thanks to the supernatural world's great leap forward into democracy and multiculturalism. "Once I came home," I

218 | LEANNE LEEDS

explained, "I got that owl on my birthday. He claims to be the goddess Athena's owl, gifted to me because I was chosen for a purpose."

"Claims?" Archie asked snidely.

Madame Margo gasped. "So you're a chosen one?"

"I'm not sure what that means," I said, shrugging. "Every now and then, a star card will turn over during one of my sister Ami's readings. The person whose star card is flipped over is in danger from some unnamed doom, and I'm supposed to keep that doom from happening."

"What kind of doom?" Captain Harmon asked.

"Death, Cap," Emma told him. "They're marked for death. Remember that actress? The one that got kidnapped from the parrot place?" Captain Harmon nodded. "She'd been to the Ardens for a reading, and the magic star card thing flipped over."

"That's how Emma and I met," I added.

"Are you telling me someone wants to kill Jason?" Lillian asked, her voice shaking. She reached toward Jason's shoulder and rested a hand lightly on him. "Why would anyone want to kill Jason? He doesn't even live here. He doesn't have anything to do with any of this."

"Are you sure?" I asked her.

"Hey, now," Jason said defensively. "What's that supposed to mean?"

I waved a hand to dismiss his concern. "Relax. We don't know at this point what any of this is. We know Bernie isn't acting like himself, two houses have burned down, and Margo's assistant over there sounds like a cult member newly sworn to the fire people."

"You know, I don't like you all that much!" Jinny jumped to her feet and yelled at me. "Jared was right! You have a bad attitude, and you're a jerk!"

I only knew one Jared.

Just one.

I had to have misheard.

"Who?" I asked quietly.

"Jared!"

That's what I thought she said.

What would the assistant to one of the top psychics in Cassandra be doing talking to Forkbridge PD's forensic examiner? "Jared Upton? Do you know Jared Upton?"

Jinny blinked and drew back like a cobra ready to strike. "Um. No. It's another Jared Upton." We stared at the girl. "A totally different Jared Upton."

If this girl was the Machiavellian linchpin to this plot, the Cassandran conspirators were in a lot of trouble.

I turned to Emma. "Jared knew my outfit was a military outfit. No one outside of the paranormal world would know this is a military uniform." At least, not unless they'd visited the paranormal world. "It surprised the hell out of me at the time, but I didn't think about it."

"Doesn't he smoke?" Captain Harmon asked. "I could swear he smokes like a chimney. The guy always smells like a used ashtray when he comes in my office."

"What does that have to do with anything?" Jason asked.

"Guru Bernie smokes now," his mother told him, her hand still clutching his shoulder. "All the time. He never smoked before. And you know we don't smoke, son. Tobacco is sacred. We don't abuse it like that."

UPTON COULD BE A SHAPESHIFTER, I reasoned.

Though I had to admit—that was a heck of a jump from his name coming up unexpectedly and his being aware of a fact he had no reason to know.

Still...

Shapeshifter lore is old. Metis, the mother of the goddess Athena, could transform herself into anything she desired. According to legend, Zeus tricked her into changing into a fly and then swallowed her. She gave birth to Athena inside Zeus' head thanks to his betrayal.

Speaking of Zeus, he repeatedly transformed himself to cheat on Hera. Hera turned his harem of mistresses into a bunch of stuff, too, in a jealous rivalry worthy of a Jerry Springer episode.

While the most well known shapeshifters were were-animals—animals that could also appear humanoid when they desired to—there were some shapeshifters who, like Metis, could change into whatever they wanted to. The Navajo Indians told tales of skinwalkers, a type of witch who can turn into, possess, or disguise themselves as animals.

Technically, humans are a form of animal.

"Why didn't you tell me that Jared guy recognized your uniform?" I looked down to find Archie staring up at me, his wings bent in a judgmental arm-cross mimic. "You don't think to tell me these things?" The owl's big, wide eyes stared up at me.

"Not for nothing, but you weren't interested in anything going on with anyone until the star card flipped over and glowed." He blinked. "You've made it clear you're not my familiar. You're a temporary alliance that flares to life when the goddess decides someone needs to be saved, and then as soon as the situation is over, you go off and do your own thing." Another blink. "So, you tell me—should I have told you?"

Archie unruffled his feathers and blinked furiously.

"Besides, maybe you're the threat to Jason. You're the only one that's attacked him this week, as far as I know."

"I was interested in saving you from that moron's proposal," Archie snapped, pointing his wing across the room toward Jason. "I wasn't doing my own thing. I was following you to make sure you didn't do something stupid."

"Like what?" I asked. "Go out on a date with a nice guy? Is that stupidity?"

A deep voice interrupted our disagreement before Archie could respond. "The owl attacked me because I was going to ask you out?"

Jason Bishop was standing right next to me.

Fantastic.

Jason had been on the other side of the room, deep in conversation with the captain, his mother, Margo, and Emma. Somehow, he crossed the entire room silently enough to overhear the exact part of the conversation I didn't want him to hear.

I tried to decide what to say to him, how to deflect—but I just went with the truth in the end. "Yes. Yes, he did," I admitted.

Jason half-smiled as he slipped into one of the chairs around the table. "So, you think I'm a nice guy, then? I don't know whether to be flattered or suspect your opinion of me might be the kiss of death for any eventual invitation I extend."

"I'm not sure I'd be joking about kisses of death if I were in your situation," I told him solemnly. "The star card? It's not a joke. It's only flipped over five times, and each time the people it flipped for were in grave danger."

He leaned back in the chair. "I'm confident you'll be able to protect me. After all, a goddess chose you for the job, and from what I remember in college about Athena? She's pretty smart." Jason smiled wider. "By the way, you're surprisingly down to earth for a demigod."

I sat down in the chair next to him and

shrugged. "I'm not a demigod. My mother's a witch, but she's mortal. She claims my father was a CIA agent or a spy or something. So, an interesting human, probably. But definitely mortal."

"As far as you know," he pointed out. "Have you ever met him?"

No, I hadn't met my father. But this was not a conversation I wanted to have in the middle of crazy town. "Do you really want to talk about this right now?"

"Is there anything I can do about the other situation?" He reached out and scratched Archie on the head without warning. "If you're going to guard me, I figured we should get to know each other better. That's all I was trying to do when this raptor decided to get in the way, you know."

The owl froze, taken aback by the audacity, and for a split second, I feared the star card really had flipped over for Jason because Archie was about to murder him. Instead, the owl raised its head and gaped at me, its menacing presence palpable. "Stop. Him. Before I snap his fingers off like peppermint sticks."

"Um, owls don't like to be petted," I told Jason, and he dropped his hand immediately, shooting Archie a look of guilt and apology. "Thanks.

They're not pets. And this one is even more independent than a regular owl."

"So what now, Astra Arden, almost-demigod and chosen of the goddess Athena?" Jason stared at me with the oddest expression. It was a mixture of calm acceptance and poise, resolute confidence I envied a little bit. "Are you my bodyguard for the remainder of the starry death alert, then?"

"Basically, yes," I said, nodding.

"So, what do I do now?"

Don't die?

"Well, I've had folks that knew and folks that didn't know. The ones that knew and cooperated were certainly a bit easier to keep alive. So, your cooperation would be greatly appreciated."

He snorted. "Have you failed to keep someone alive, Astra?" he asked.

"I don't fail," I retorted.

"That's good to know," Jason responded, nodding. "I already feel safer."

"The simplest thing to do would be to keep you at my mother's house for the time being back in Forkbridge," I explained, leaning forward. "The house has been warded, and if this is a magical situation, that will help."

Jason visibly balked and then shook his head

no. "As much as I value the security of hiding, I am not a coward."

"Look, I never said you were. It's just—"

"I'll follow you wherever you go. I'll even make sure to stand behind you if that's what you want," he added. "But I'm not hiding. My mother's house burned down, and my hometown is in the grips of some odd conspiracy. I'm not heading to the next town over to sit on a couch watching Netflix while the rest of you figure this out."

I pulled out my phone. It was after ten.

Spotting my look, Emma called out to me. "What do you want to do?"

I rolled my shoulders and looked at Emma, then at Archie. "Well, it's late, and it's going to be hard to weave in and out of the drunk tourist clutch out there and stay on guard. I'd also like to talk to Ami, find out what she saw in Jason's reading. Get some sleep. Regroup in the morning."

Emma turned toward the mayor. "What can we help you with before we go?"

"Well, Margo needs to find a place to stay for the night," Lillian Thornton said, gesturing toward the other psychic. "Jinny, do you—" The mayor looked around. "Where's Jinny?"

Margo blinked and looked around. "Jinny?"

Just then, Joe Gillespie walked into the room from the back with fresh cups of coffee. "Jinny?" he asked, gesturing with the piping hot coffee toward the back of the storefront. "She went out the back about ten minutes ago. Said she had something to do."

"WELL, I was going to question her!" Emma complained, throwing her arms up in the air. "First, I wanted to figure out what to do about Bishop and the star card crisis! Someone potentially getting killed seemed more important!"

"Put your hands back on the wheel!" I warned her.

Emma put her hands back on the wheel.

Captain Harmon volunteered to sleep on the porch chairs outside Guru Bernie's house since the mayor had to stay there. Lillian said there was no particular rule saying Margo couldn't bunk with her, so the second most powerful psychic headed back to the bungalow with the mayor.

Jason Bishop, Emma, and I headed back to Forkbridge in her old, creaky Chevy Malibu.

Since Jason's life was in danger, the safest course of immediate action was to head back to Arden House. We'd get some sleep and go over Ami's information in the morning.

"This is going to get a whole lot harder tomorrow," Jason murmured as he glanced out the window at the tourists heading back to their hotel rooms, tents, RVs, and B&Bs. "Tomorrow's Friday, and Halloween is Saturday—which is a weekend. The town is going to be crawling with tourists, and no one's going to have time to talk to us."

"They'll talk to us," I said with confidence.

Emma slammed on the brakes as a pedestrian started across the street despite our light being green. The man jumped back and waved his fist at her. Emma pulled out her badge and held it up. His angry shouts stopped instantly and he hurried out of her way. Emma accelerated slowly through the intersection.

"It's crawling with tourists now," Emma said, glancing in the rearview mirror.

"This is nothing compared to tomorrow, and it'll be even worse Saturday." I turned to face Jason and spotted the concern evident in his expression.

"What?"

"Why would they want to kill you?" I asked him.

"Well, since we don't know who 'they' are, I couldn't tell you. Like I said, I don't live in Cassandra anymore, and I'm not really a full-fledged member of the community. I'm not a threat to anybody."

"Does someone have to have it out for him, you think?" Emma asked.

I wasn't sure how to reply to that. "What do you mean?"

"Well, the first case we had, someone didn't really want to kill that woman, not exactly. It's just that circumstances lined up to put her life in danger, right?" I nodded. "Could that be happening here? Could Jason's life be in danger because he will put himself in a situation where his life is threatened? Like, say, protecting his mother?"

"It's possible. Anything's possible."

Jason shrugged. "Maybe that's it. I just can't figure out who'd want to hurt me. The people I knew in Cassandra are all still there. I have friends from high school. Well, high school years, in any case."

"I think you're just going to be in the wrong place at the wrong time," Emma continued, pulling into a parking space in front of my house. "Or, you know, maybe you're going to be kidnapped and used to manipulate your mother. Someone could use you for their own gain."

"What do you mean?" I asked, turning around to face Emma. "Like leverage? Or—"

"I'd rather walk around with a target on my back than stay here and hide," Jason said with a grim expression. He sighed heavily. "C'mon, let's get some sleep. All these questions will still be there in the morning."

CHAPTER FOURTEEN

*A*rden House was buzzing with excited activity the following morning. No pall of doom (despite the two overnight guests being added to the breakfast table due to a death threat). "I hope you like eggs and bacon," Aunt Gwennie—ever the family manager—said with a smile. "Thea is just finishing up with the pancakes. They should be ready any minute now."

"Yes, thank you," Jason said politely. "I very much appreciate your hospitality."

"Of course he likes bacon and eggs," Ayla said, her tone devoid of the resentment or sadness Archie claimed the thirteen-year-old displayed the night before. "And everyone enjoys pancakes, right?"

"Ayla, wait until Jason gets some coffee in him before you start bothering him," I advised my sister. She came to a complete stop, looked at me, and then turned away. "Hey, Ayla, come on. What's wrong?"

The happy chatter that had engulfed the sunny alcove gave way to a dark and foreboding silence. Ayla stormed out of the room, and my sister, Ami, stalked silently into the kitchen behind her like a flank guard.

I raised my eyebrow at Aunt Gwennie. "Was it something I said?"

"Ayla had a pretty difficult night last night, Astra." My aunt arranged the blue-flower-patterned plates on the table as she spoke. "I understand why you left her here. It was late, after all, and there was drinking in Cassandra. But she was excited to be a part of this case, and she struggled to deal with her disappointment when she wasn't."

I held up my hands. "But what is she mad at me for? Mom never would have let me take her, even if I'd asked."

"Well, I know that. And you know that." Aunt Gwennie folded her hands in front of her and sighed. "But all Ayla knows, dear, is you didn't bother to ask."

As much as I enjoyed getting to know my sisters, the complexities of dealing with teenage and barely-beyond-teenage witches tested my nerves. I'd led soldiers, trackers, and even an assassin or two. None had been as perplexing as the teenage witch brigade that evenly divided the house.

Three adults—my mother, Aunt Gwennie, and me.

Three teenagers—Ayla, Althea, and Ami.

And an owl.

Though the owl seemed wrapped up in his own stuff lately.

"What's on the agenda for today?" Emma asked, her eyes growing wide as Aunt Gwennie placed a warm maple syrup pitcher on the table. "After breakfast, I mean." Jason raised his eyebrow at Emma. "What? That's real maple syrup, dude."

Jason's eyes sparkled with amusement. "Absolutely. Real maple syrup trumps my life being in danger any day of the week. It's not like there's a clock ticking on the situation." Emma and I exchanged a glance that Jason caught. He looked back and forth between us, the amusement fading. "Unless there is?"

I sat down. "Generally, from the time the star

card flips over, we have about seventy-two hours until whatever is going to happen will happen," I explained, gesturing toward a chair. "It's not an exact science, though. It could be a bit more or a bit less."

"And I flipped a card over for you at about nine-thirty last night," Ami announced. She walked over and placed a heaping plate of bacon down next to Jason. "Twelve hours already passed."

"That means we need to unravel the threat to you quickly." My mother's voice rang out from the stairwell as she descended like a queen ready to entertain. "Jason. It's good to finally properly meet you."

I stared at her, confused.

She met him last night.

Well, okay, she saw him last night. They weren't, like, formally introduced, and Mom was asleep when we all got back from Cassandra.

But still.

"My name is Minerva Arden." Mom bowed her head as if greeting a visiting dignitary. Standing straight again, she added, "I am Astra's mother."

Jason stood up from the table and leaned in my mother's direction with a ceremonial formality. "It's a pleasure and an honor to meet you, Ms. Arden. Thank you for your hospitality and assistance with my mother's issue—as well as, clearly, my own."

My mother beamed.

To keep my eyes from rolling out of my head, I closed them and pinched the bridge of my nose. I will not say it felt like a scene from *Downton Abbey*, but it was perilously close.

"Astra looks irritated," Ayla announced.

I opened my eyes. "I'm not irritated," I told her.

"Well, *I* am," the kid snapped back. "In case you were wondering."

"Ayla," my mother said sharply. "I don't think this is the time or place to air family grievances. We have guests."

Ayla sighed, and her shoulders slumped forward.

"Ayla." She looked up and met my eyes. I jerked my head toward the other people in the room. "We'll talk later, okay?"

"Yeah, sure. Whatever," she mumbled sullenly.

My mother's expression turned stormy. "Astra, you're in the middle of a star card case. Jason Bishop's life is in danger, and we've all got to discover who's burning down homes in

Cassandra." My mother stared with unrelenting dissatisfaction at Ayla, who returned her look with fury. "We also—as if that was not enough—need to locate the Cassandran ghosts and help them if they need it." Ayla finally looked down, her face hot. "I think Ayla's teenage grievances can wait. Whatever longings or frustrations she has? I have no doubt they will still be there when we are done."

Ami squeezed Ayla's shoulder in sympathy, but my youngest sibling angrily shook off her hand.

"THE READING INDICATED that whoever is setting the fires, they are...how do I say this? A furnace of ambition," Ami explained after breakfast. My sister always had a very poetic way of explaining things she saw in readings, and for a moment I wondered if the reference to fire and heat was meaningful. "They are attempting to reclaim a form of immortality they believe was taken from them."

"Taken? Taken by who? My mother? Psychics?" Jason asked.

Ami shrugged. "Without someone asking for

the reading? I don't have anyone to work through the hints with." She held up the cards. "I can get indications, but no specifics. Desires or wants or things they're angry with? I can see all that. But the querent—"

Jason swallowed the coffee that remained in his cup and then placed it on the table. "Sorry, the what?"

"*One who seeks*," I told Jason. "It's the person who questions the oracle for information. They're at the foundation of the reading, the block everything else builds on. If you don't have that, the reading can be a little unclear."

"Exactly," Ami said, nodding. "Without a querent to anchor the information on, it's like getting snippets of a situation without being able to get the full context. Pieces of a puzzle without knowing what the big picture is."

Jason tilted his head. "But you're the one who asked, right? So wouldn't that make you the querent?"

"Ami is the oracle, Jason," my mother told him (with absolutely no qualms about upgrading their relationship to first names). "She can ask to be shown information about others, people she has no connection to. That information, however, is much more difficult to tie together into a cohesive picture."

"It's like eavesdropping on a conversation or watching two people have a discussion when you can't quite hear what they're saying," Aunt Gwennie said, looking up from her knitting. "You can get information—from their body language, their gestures, their expressions—but you may not know who or what it applies to."

Ami nodded. "That's as good an analogy as any. So, I know snippets. No big picture."

"You know, someone striving for immortality sounds an awful lot like the people I used to work for," I said, sitting back and crossing my arms. "In the past few days, I've had two people mention that my outfit was a military uniform. The only people that know this is a military uniform are people that know me well, or people that lived in Paranormopolis, or people that are familiar with the paranormal world."

"Who called you out on your uniform?" Althea asked, frowning.

"Yesterday morning, it was Jared Upton."

"The retired forensic investigator? The snotty one that works part-time?" my mother asked.

I nodded. "He's a cantankerous old—"

My aunt clicked her tongue. "Let's watch it

with the classifications of old people, young lady," Aunt Gwennie interrupted. "Those flippant statements have a way of coming back to haunt you later in life."

"And they have a way of insulting your elders now," my mother murmured.

"Look, this guy would be obnoxious at any age. He's just rude and patronizing, and one of these misogynistic men trapped in another era," I told them. "We've never exactly been the best of friends, but his attitude seems to have gotten worse of late."

"He has been a little more snippy than usual," Emma admitted. "And Jinny mentioned him. That just seemed odd."

"The thing that really caught my attention, though, is that he smokes. I know it seems small. If it was just him being kind of a jerk, okay, whatever. He's a jerk." I held up my hands. "If it was just that he knew my uniform was from the paranormal military? That's a little weirder, but nothing to freak out about. The fact that he smokes and the guru is now a chain-smoking, cantankerous old man instead of the sweet health-nut he used to be?"

We all fell silent, thinking.

"Astra, dear," my mother asked. "You said

there was a second person that was able to identify your uniform?"

"Edgar," I answered. "He's one of the fire tender guys, and he passed a really suspicious note to a guy telling us some information." I looked at Jason. "Jason seemed to know him. Can you think of any reason your friend would know where my uniform came from?"

Jason seemed uncomfortable as he nodded back. "Astra, your mother could probably speak to it more than I could. The spiritualists are wary of you witches. I mean, it's built into the belief system. As a consequence, some of the committees study your people. So, they could know. I mean, it wouldn't surprise me if Edgar knew that way. It doesn't necessarily mean anything."

"But the note?" Emma asked.

Jason didn't answer.

"What kind of agreement do you have with these Cassandran people, anyway, Mom?" I asked, annoyed that I spent so many years ignoring my mother when she clearly knew some stuff. "Why would you and the guru have to come to an agreement about anything?"

"The town—Cassandra—descends from witch-finders, Astra," Aunt Gwennie answered for Mom. "Witch Lake was not named that to be cute or as some type of honorific to witches." My aunt looked up from her knitting. "The lake got its name because of the poor souls that were drowned in it trying to prove they weren't one of us."

Ayla glared at Jason with repugnance. "Geez, man, what kind of town did you come from?"

Jason looked back at her but didn't respond— which impressed me. Ayla's attitude was off the charts today. Not sure I could bite my tongue in the face of that sneer.

"Almost all towns have a history, Ayla," Althea told our younger sister. "Society has evolved in the last hundred years, you know. You go back far enough, you'll always find bad people. Or at least people that we perceive now as bad."

"That doesn't mean we excuse atrocities in history, though," Ami told Ayla with a frown and then turned toward Althea. "And I should point out, this isn't history. Bad people are running around in Cassandra today. Right now. As we sit here talking."

"I think we might be getting a little off track here," I said, leaning forward. "Mom, does the agreement that you signed with the guru have anything to do with what's going on here? You're the only one that knows what's in it. So, you tell us—do we need to worry about it? Think about it? Read it?"

"I'm happy to share it with you. It's not a secret. It's just an agreement between two leaders not to go into the other's sphere of influence, I suppose." Mom tilted her head and tapped her fingers on the table. "If you want to know the truth, it's more political than anything else. As long as we don't cross over into the other person's territory, each of us agrees not to attack."

"Not to attack what?" Emma asked.

"Anything. Each other. Each other's people," Mom responded. "It's nothing more than signed assurances that the two of us will stay out of each other's way and out of each other's business." She motioned toward a bookshelf with books and paper. "You're welcome to look, but I don't think it has anything to do with what's going on here with the burned houses or Astra being identified as a military witch...I truly just don't see how it does."

Jason and I looked at one another. "Has Edgar always lived in Cassandra?" I asked him. He nodded. "Okay. His knowledge of my uniform might be from some kind of witch education in Cassandra. I can buy that. That doesn't explain

Jared Upton knowing what it was—and Emma's right. Jinny strongly implied she'd spoken to Jared and he was even somehow influencing or advising her."

"Yeah, that was pretty weird," Emma agreed. "Jason may know Edgar from way back, but Jared is new here in Forkbridge. Well, relatively." She leaned back and scrutinized the ceiling fan. "He's only been here a couple of years. Dude claimed to be retired from a big city department back east, but if he's a witch, I guess faking a history to get hired wouldn't be that hard."

Several of us nodded.

"Okay, then while you guys head back over to Cassandra, I can start digging into Upton's history," Althea said with determination. "Everyone leaves a trail these days. We'll know if he is who he says he is by the end of the day."

"Ayla," I said, turning to the thirteen-year-old, "I need you to start calling out to any ghosts you can and getting whatever information you can about the disappearance of the Cassandran spirits. I want to know rumors, what they are claiming to each other is going on, why they're avoiding the place. Everything."

"So you're not taking me over there again? Seriously?" Ayla hung on to her spoiled brat attitude with a furious, untiring zeal. "You said I could work on this case!"

"You are working on the case," I told her calmly.

Ami reached out again for Ayla. "Sis, we are all working on the case. No matter where we are. I'm sitting here and doing readings. Althea will start hacking things all over the place to find out the information Emma and Astra need. You're going to call the ghosts here, and you're probably gonna need Mom's help to do that," Ami pointed out, glancing at my mother. "We are all doing what we can, what we need to do—"

"I'm going to be locked in this house until the day I die," Ayla muttered as she slammed against the back of the chair. Then, her expression sourly petulant, she added, "I'm never gonna get to do anything fun. Ever!"

My mother opened her mouth to say something, but Aunt Gwennie put her hand gently on Mom's arm. "Let the girls do what they can do," she whispered.

To anyone listening, it sounded like my aunt was urging my mother not to ground Ayla, but I sensed her comment was far more than that.

The three older Arden girls—myself included, obviously—were working well together on this case. I think my aunt hoped that our example would do more to help Ayla understand how her attitude was detrimental than anything my mother could say outright.

My mother took a deep breath and nodded. "You girls seem to have the situation under control for now. And I think you're correct. I can be of use by assisting Ayla with the call to the spirit world." Mom's tone was uncharacteristically unassertive, and her posture was proud but compliant. She caught my eye. "Since this is your case, we will do what needs to be done here and will contact you as soon as we know anything." Mom turned to Emma. "Emma, please make sure all of us have your cell phone number as well. Just in case Astra is too busy to speak to us."

"Got it," Emma told her, pulling out her phone.

"And Jason, please be careful."

Jason nodded.

"Oh, no, not a chance," I told Jason. "I am not going into that Halloween-themed crazy town dressed in a costume! Are you kidding me?"

"Today is the day before Halloween. Folks in town will be in a costume. Every tourist, every visitor, and half the people that live there," Jason insisted. "If we go back there the way we were dressed yesterday, everyone will see us coming from a mile away."

"Especially you, Ms. Black Widow outfit person," Emma said.

"You make fun of me all the time that I look like I'm in costume, anyway. So why do I have to wear a costume if you think I look like I am in a costume?"

"Because you only wear that one thing, Astra," Jason told me earnestly. "You've been in the news. You and Emma are the famous detective/psychic pair that closed cold cases twenty years old. Everyone knows who you are and what you look like. And if they didn't before yesterday? I guarantee you they know who you are now."

Emma glanced at Jason. "You think people are going to be on guard today? Not want to talk to us?"

"I think since the two of you showed up in Cassandra, whoever the guilty party is? They've most likely been solely concerned with ensuring that you don't talk to the people you need to talk to." Jason's words had an unmistakable ring of truth to them. "If you both disguise yourselves, you can talk to people, and no one will know who you are."

I gave Jason a caustic glare. "A town of psychics won't recognize us because of some costumes? That doesn't make sense, does it?" I nodded like my point was the best argument against these nut bars getting me in some Halloween costume.

"The town of *mediums* won't know it's you because of some costumes. There won't be any ghosts around to tell them any differently," Jason explained.

Oh. Right.

Damn it.

"I can't believe I'm letting you talk me into this." I gave him the most vicious glare I could come up with. "Fine. What kind of Halloween costumes should we wear to blend in? Is there a theme, or anything goes?"

"Anything goes, and I got just the thing," Jason smiled. "How do you feel about anime?"

"I felt just fine about anime until you said that," I answered grumpily.

CHAPTER FIFTEEN

struggled to climb out of the car and muttered a string of curses at Jason. "I can't believe I let you talk me into this. It's hot as Hades in here, and I can barely see. How am I supposed to investigate if I can't see anyone?" Jason had let me borrow one of his cosplay costumes, some dude called No-Face who—despite the name—had quite a heavy face, so big I had to look out of its mouth hole. "Not to mention I look like a black blob that someone stuck a face on."

Jason helped me the rest of the way with a fur-covered hand. "That's the whole point of the costume, Astra. No one's going to recognize you in that." He shifted my face mask up slightly, and it was instantly more comfortable. "It covers you from head to toe."

Jason—at least as hot as I was in a Chewbacca costume that had seen better days—had been right about this being cosplay day in the town of Cassandra. I'd once chased a fairy fugitive in San Diego right into Comic-Con, and the people there hadn't looked all that much different from the people wandering the streets here.

By the way, do you know how hard it is to find a rogue fairy in Comic-Con?

It's hard. Really hard.

"Okay, I think we should split up," Emma said, crossing her arms. "While I'm pretty happy to be in a much more comfortable costume than either of you, if the three of us walk around together, everyone's gonna know who you are, anyway."

Emma had grabbed a knee-length raincoat from Aunt Gwennie and a magnifying glass from Althea. She announced she was Shirley Holmes, Sherlock Holmes' descendant.

Yeah, she wasn't really in costume.

"Where are you going to go first?" I asked her.

"I'm going to check in with Joe Gillespie at the visitors' center and see what the schedule is for today. Then I'm going to try to find Jinny. I want to know how she knows Jared Upton and what Jared said to her."

I nodded and turned toward Jason. "We should probably stop in and check with your mother to see if anything else happened. You should, too, Emma—unless you talked to the captain this morning?" I raised my eyebrow.

But, of course, Emma couldn't see my eyebrow raise.

"I talked to him earlier this morning. Nothing else burned down, if that's what you mean," Emma said, watching the excited tourists walk by with...

...something.

Food booths were set up along either side of the street, and everything had the air of a carnival. I shuddered as I read the sign nearest us —how on earth can you deep-fry butter?

"They really set this place up overnight." Emma spotted the deep-fried butter booth. "I'm going to have to try that before we go."

"Surely you must be joking."

"Don't call me Shirley," she told me absentmindedly and then snort-laughed at her own joke. "Get it? Don't call me Shirley? Ah, I crack myself up sometimes."

"I'm glad to know my imminent death isn't

really something to be concerned about," Jason told her. I wasn't sure if he had an itch or winced, but he full-body twitched in response. I'm betting he winced. "I didn't know you had such an antiquated humor, Detective."

Emma glared with offended sulkiness. "Did you just call me old and uncool all in one sentence? You were an English major, weren't you?"

"I was not, no, and I would never do that—"

Jason stopped talking abruptly as Bill Platt crossed three feet in front of us, deep in conversation with Serena Bliss. Neither of them had spotted Emma, so she turned around, back to them, to ensure they did not see her.

"Go," she whispered. "I'll text you when I have anything."

JASON and I took off after them as nonchalantly as we could manage. We got within hearing distance after a few significant but subtle steps.

"Considering the mayor invited outside law enforcement to investigate, Serena, I need assurances that no one's going to say anything about the missing gasoline," Bill suddenly snapped like a gunshot. "I don't need any more problems than I already have during Halloween, and I don't want to be involved in whatever this investigation is."

"Whatever what investigation is, Bill?" Serena demanded coldly without slowing her pace. "Are we talking about the Forkbridge police investigation, the fire tenders' investigation, a game of Clue? You'll have to be more specific if you want me to do something for you." She practically oozed condescension.

"I just want to make sure you're going to keep your mouth shut," Bill said as they stepped up on the curb. He politely extended his hand to help her, but she slapped it away. Bill dropped it and glowered. "You have a way of running your mouth and making things far worse than they need to be. And I know you and Jason used to be involved."

Serena Bliss and Jason what now?

If Jason was worried about what I'd overheard, or with my knowing he and Serena used to be a couple, he didn't show it. Of course, he could have been sweating and raging in the Chewbacca suit, and I would have missed it.

"Who I used to date, Bill, is none of your business. You reported the stolen gas, I wrote the report up, and I will bring it to the guru and the mayor after the Halloween festival. It's not important right now," she responded, her tone remaining tense. "If you want it dealt with faster than that, I'm going to have to report it to whoever the mayor tells me to report it to." Serena came to a halt and turned to face the owner of the filling station. "And I'm going to have to report that you didn't want the police to know, so think carefully about what you say to me next."

"You're such a goody-two-shoes," Bill sneered.

"That's usually what's required in this position," Serena shot back.

Jason and I stood back and watched as the two confronted each other. Unconcerned revelers went by, holding mugs of eerie-looking liquids. Bill's nostrils flared as he inhaled and exhaled deeply. Minutes seemed to pass without a word being spoken.

"I don't like you, and I don't trust you," Bill told Serena finally.

"That feeling, Bill? It's absolutely mutual. I promise you." She stepped back and held her hands out palms up. "But I have a role in this town, and you are a member of the community. So I will do my best for you, and I will do my best to do what you have asked." Serena suddenly smiled faintly. "I fear, however, the investigators may be aware of the missing gas already."

Bill's jaw dropped. "What are you talking about? How?"

"Like I said, it's just a feeling." Serena let her hands drop and tilted her head. "We've gotten more discreet in the month since the spirits left. We've learned to conceal ourselves. Of course, everyone believes those secrets are safe because no ghosts are roaming around telling people what other people are doing." Serena smiled. "But we're not practiced in the art of deception, Bill. So even without the ghosts, I suspect nothing will stay hidden for long."

He looked at her carefully. "You holy people are so weird."

Serena bowed her head. "But we are often right." She looked up and smiled at the agitated man. "There's something I have to do. You have a good day, Bill." Her tone was unmistakably dismissive.

Bill Platt took a deep breath, turned on his heel, and walked away from Serena.

A minute or so passed, but the woman didn't move from her spot. Finally, Serena turned and looked directly at us. "Did you two get all that?"

"You knew it was me the whole time, didn't you," Jason said to Serena, and it wasn't a question. "I forgot that you've seen my costumes."

Serena replied by pointing at me. "I've worn No-Face." She crossed the sidewalk to join us. "Let's just say I suspected it was you when you began trailing us. I was sure once you both stopped to listen to my conversation with Bill Platt." She glanced at me. "Is that the witch or the detective?"

"Astra's in that costume," Jason responded. Serena flashed a brief smile. "What? What's the smile for?"

"It's good to know my instincts are still intact. I pegged her as more your type than the detective," she told him, her tone lightly amused. Jason responded with a nod as if this was an understandable viewpoint. "I'm impressed your mother hasn't run her off yet. Perhaps people can change."

I thrust my head forward to interrupt the dialogue getting far too personal, and with a bang, I slammed it into the mask.

Ow.

"Um, Jason and I are not dating. I don't know where anyone is getting the idea that Jason and I are dating, but we're not dating," I explained in a muffled voice from behind several layers of black cotton. "We're just running partners. In fact, this is the first time I've ever seen him outside of anything having to do with running."

I started to hear myself and realized I was protesting excessively. Or, at the very least, that it would possibly appear I was protesting excessively. I couldn't seem to quit talking about Jason and me not dating—which, I realized, gave the impression I was trying to hide that we were dating.

Chewbacca stared at me.

"Well, now that we've cleared that up," Serena said, rubbing her hands together, "I have a few things I need to get done today. Your mother is in the guru's house." She moved in the opposite direction. "I'm sorry, but I have to leave to give the seeker speech."

Jason tilted his head. "Really? The guru isn't doing that this year?"

"For a variety of reasons, we've decided that he might not be the greatest fit for the job right now. He's also required elsewhere since he is the only one who has access to the ghosts."

They nodded knowingly while I remained baffled.

"What's the seeker speech?" I asked, lightly

lifting the mask upward and peering at Serena through the small oval mouth hole. "And what's the deal about the stolen gas?"

Serena glanced at her watch. "I really have to go."

"Why don't we come with you," Jason said, stepping forward. His movement encouraged Serena to walk. "I can explain to Astra what the seeker speech is, and she can watch it firsthand since it generally isn't very long." Serena nodded. "Once you're done, you should have a few minutes to talk to us."

WE STEPPED around the corner and found ourselves in a yurt full of tourists vividly dressed in costumes. A considerable number of them clutched pamphlets, their faces shining with excitement. As Jason moved toward the rear of the room, I leaned forward and inspected the front page of a soggy brochure clasped in the fist of a woman costumed as Cleopatra.

SO YOU WANT TO MOVE TO CASSANDRA?

"All these people want to move here?" I whispered to Jason.

He nodded. "Every year, a large number of people decide to leave their lives behind so they can find themselves in the psychic town. The spiritual life they tasted on vacation just wasn't enough." Jason made air quotes around *psychic town* and *find themselves* and *spiritual life*.

"But I thought almost no one moves here. At least that's what my mother claimed."

"She's right. Almost no one does. It's an appealing concept for people, especially those that would choose to come here on their vacation, but once they're told what living here entails?" Jason chuckled. "Anyway, we found it is easier to deal with them all at once. As opposed to having people in the throes of some kind of relocation ecstasy run around and harass everyone in the town."

Serena cleared her throat and launched into a wonderful description of living in Cassandra. "We are all brothers and sisters, brought together and brought up together to love one another. To always be there for each other, and to always be there for those that come to seek our help," she told the assembled crowd in a kind voice, her eyes sparkling with happiness. "We can understand why you would want to move here,

260 | LEANNE LEEDS

but before you do, we feel there are some things you should know."

By the time Serena mentioned the town depends on ghosts to alert them to fire, half the attendees had got up and walked away. She lost a few more when she mentioned the required fifty-percent annual tithe, more again at the requirement to use the religious leaders in place of a secular court.

When it was revealed that the leadership's consent was needed to hold any job in or out of Cassandra, the remainder of the group scurried out.

"Okay, you understand this sounds like a cult, don't you?" I took off the upper half of my costume, feeling the rush of cool air on my heated flesh. "Everything you just stated, everything you outlined—you don't have complete control over your lives. I mean, isn't this illegal?"

Serena and Jason exchanged looks. "Astra, I told you no one was obligated to stay. But it's not something you can give up, you know? I could return here if I ever needed assistance. You know what I mean?"

"You said that twice. No," I told him flatly. "I don't know."

"This town is communal, Ms. Arden. That's how it was intended. So that no one is ever alone. Some people flourish here, while others want to be more self-sufficient and less reliant on others." Serena cast a short peek at Jason before averting her gaze. "I understand how it appears from the outside, and I recognize that some of our rules and interdependencies appear strange, but we like it this way. It works for us."

Jason gave a kind smile. "Like I said, Astra, this place isn't without its charms." Then his smile faded into a frown. "Though I can't recall the last time something like this happened here. The fires and someone being out to kill my mother? It's crazy."

"What do you mean, someone wants the mayor dead?" Serena looked shocked at the concept. "How do you know someone wants the mayor dead?"

"I probably shouldn't have said that. I don't know that. It's just a feeling I have, I guess." He didn't mention the star card, or the possibility that someone might want him dead. "But her house burned down—"

"So did Madame Margo's," Serena pointed out. "Are you saying that someone wants both of them dead?"

"What happens to their homes?" I interrupted suddenly.

Serena Bliss frowned. "I'm not sure I understand your question."

"Well, I just listened to you explain the town is communal, so your church owns all the homes and all the land. Everything is held in trust, right?"

Jason and Serena nodded.

"So what happens to Margo and the mayor now?" I asked the two. "Does the town pay for their homes to be rebuilt? Do they come together to rebuild them like an Amish barn raising? How does your socialist hippie conclave deal with that?"

"Well, that didn't seem insulting at all," Jason observed sarcastically.

Serena ignored him. "Normally, the town would get together and rebuild their homes. Well, the members of the town that have the skills. The cost of the materials would come out of the town building fund."

"Where do they stay until their homes are rebuilt?" I asked.

"I know Madame Margo rented an apartment from Bob and Jane Aurora," Serena told me, gesturing toward the entrance behind me. The three of us moved toward the angled yurt entryway.

I glanced out toward the main thoroughfare. So, not only does Bob have the official Cassandra jeweler, he also has an apartment building? How did the new guy in town get "issued" all these income producing businesses?

"Do you see the jewelry store over there? And the floors above it?" She turned back. "That's where Margo is staying and likely, I suspect, where the mayor will stay after Halloween." Serena fidgeted and looked nervously at Jason. "If she's still the mayor, in any case."

Jason turned and looked at Serena. "What do you mean if she is still the mayor?"

"Jason," Serena said…and paused.

"Tell me, Serena."

She took a deep breath and then went on. "There's a petition right now to recall your mother. I'm sorry. I know you and I have had our differences, and your mother and I have had our differences, but I…I didn't want to be the one to tell you."

Jason said nothing in response.

"Who started the petition?" I asked Serena.

Serena paused once more and then said, "I did."

CHAPTER SIXTEEN

*J*ason—as Chewbacca—and I looked at Serena in bewilderment. He removed his mask and scratched his head, visibly concerned. "What made you start the petition?" he inquired of his ex-girlfriend. His voice sounded weird, rougher in some ways. Like he was trying not to sound angry even though he most definitely was.

Serena stared back at him as if she couldn't understand what he had said. "You've seen what's been happening here the last couple of days, Jason. If you see how it is, do you really need to ask?"

"Yes. I really need to ask." When his surprise finally passed, his eyes narrowed. The clear resemblance to his mother was unmistakable. They had the same fierce and determined expression. "Just tell me."

Serena folded her arms defiantly. "There are three people in charge of this town, Jason. Three people." She extended a hand. "You know who those three people are?"

"Guru Bernie, my mother, and you—"

"The trifecta of wisdom," she snapped, her hands clenching into fists. "Only for the past month, the guru has taken control of all the ghosts we count on for the *real* guidance. Taken them somewhere, cut us off from them." Serena stopped as if suddenly remembering where she was and scanned nearby to see whether she had been overheard. Satisfied no one was paying attention, she turned back to Jason. "And your mother, too *busy* with her new boyfriend, has just gone along with everything that happened. Questioning nothing. Until, you know, her house burned down."

A sweaty Jason frowned. "What does that have to do with your choice to—"

"My *mother* was one of those ghosts, Jason!" Serena exploded in a fury so bright it practically illuminated her face in a hazy glow. "My mother, the former guru of this town, is cut off from me!

And I can do nothing. I don't even know if she's all right. I don't have access to her guidance anymore. And do you know what power the assistant has in a situation like this? Politically, spiritually? None!"

"Hold up. A situation like what?" I asked, confused.

Serena turned as if she just remembered I was there. "Why do you care about this, witch?" Suddenly, the blaze of anger left Serena's eyes; now all that was left was a chilly, smoldering fire. "Your people hate us. They always have."

I suddenly felt a little sorry for her. "I don't hate you. Serena, I'm trying to—"

Before I could answer, she cut me off. "I am powerless—politically speaking—to address anything that's happening in the town right now. Guru Bernie acts strange, and there's nothing I can do. The mayor is distracted in a new relationship, so distracted the ghosts have disappeared, and she doesn't seem to care—and there's nothing I can do." Serena pointedly looked at her ex-boyfriend. "I am powerless to find out what's going on. And yet, it's my responsibility to try and keep this town together. To assure everyone all of these things are meant to be, that they have reasons behind them."

It was beginning to be really obvious, like a flashing neon sign, that everyone I talked to said the ghosts had disappeared. They were unreachable; no one could speak to them but the guru—and some didn't even claim that.

Robert Aurora, on the other hand, claimed they could be checked out like library books. That access was being controlled just a bit more tightly.

So far, he and the fire tenders were the *only* ones that had told me that.

Everyone else claimed they were gone.

"You don't think there are reasons behind it?" I asked her.

"I don't think the reasons are the ones I've been given by Guru Bernie, and the reasons I've given are nothing more than my attempt to make the best of a bad situation," she answered simply. "Normally, I would seek counsel with my mother. But, obviously, that's out of the question. So I did the only thing I could think to do."

"Recall my mother? Really? That's all you could think of?" Jason said.

"She's trying to remove the only person that can be replaced and hope that resolves something," I guessed. Not really knowing why I did it, I reached into my pocket and made sure the stone Ayla gave me was still there. "You think this all might be connected?"

"I do," Serena said with a nod. "Or, at the very least, I don't believe the guru is in his right mind or giving holy counsel to the town. Or me," she added bitterly.

I nodded. "And that has to do with the mayor how again?"

Serena glared at me. "Of course, *you* wouldn't understand."

"If my mother's house burning down was an accident, though, the only thing really happening is the ghosts not being around anymore," Jason reminded her. His voice was a good ten degrees colder than it had been when he'd started talking to her. "That's a religious thing, Serena. That's nothing my mother would deal with as the mayor, anyway."

Serena just looked at him. "You haven't changed," she said quietly. "You still don't understand how this town works. You believe that the rules—"

"Obviously not," Jason snapped. "I left, didn't I?"

I couldn't help but feel like I wasn't getting the whole story. I didn't understand the context of what they were talking about, and I had no idea why Serena appeared so very different now than the first day I met her. "Serena, if you're trying to remove the mayor from her position, you realize that makes *you* a bit suspicious as far as these house fires are concerned."

"I beg your pardon?" she asked me coldly.

"Well, you're trying to recall Mayor Thornton, and her house burns down. From what I understand, the most powerful psychic—"

"Medium," Serena interjected absentmindedly.

"The most powerful medium is usually the mayor. Right now, that's Jason's mother. So, following that to its most logical conclusion? Say you remove Mayor Thornton from the job." I leaned back against a pole. "The second most powerful medium in town would be the mayor, or at least run to be the mayor as a formality, right?" I nodded toward Madame Margo's home. "So that would be Margo, the medium living in the *second* house that burned down." Jason and Serena exchanged surprised glances. "That seems like a massive coincidence. When do you slip into the line of succession, I wonder?"

"I don't. Not for mayor." She paused and breathed deeply as if to calm herself. "You think someone's doing this to attack mayoral candidates?" Serena asked.

"Is there some reason burning someone's house down is a big deal in a mayoral race?" I asked.

Serena been frowning, but now her face went slack.

"The *candidacy* rules," Jason gasped. His face lost all trace of color. "Someone running for mayor of Cassandra is *required* to have a house in town. Like, literally. No one without an assigned home can run for mayor. It was done to protect the town from being run by an outsider or taken over by an outsider."

"Well, like I said—that makes you a bit suspicious," I said to Serena with a raised eyebrow. "No one would be burning down homes if there wasn't a recall election, and there's only a recall election because you started the petition."

"I swear to you, witch, I had nothing to do with any arson or any homes burning down." She extended her hand toward me. "I know what your power is. I give you permission to read me and confirm that what I say is true." I looked at her hand. "I started the petition to address problems with the town. I had no agenda beyond that."

"Okay, just hold your horses a second," I said with a shrug and waved away her extended hand. Whenever anyone volunteers eagerly to have me rummage around in their mind, I become far less concerned they're one of the bad guys. "The mayor is attacked, and the story is the 'fire spirit' wanted her house burned down or something. Then we have the next logical potential leader attacked-ish. Not enough to hurt her, but enough to push her out of the running and disqualify her as mayor. So, the obvious question is—"

"Who's the third most powerful medium?" Jason said quietly.

"Yup," I answered. "That would be the obvious question." I turned and looked at Serena. "Since you're one of the holy trifecta people, I bet you could tell me who it is. Do you guys have some sort of ranking? Some list of mediums going from most powerful to least powerful?"

"We do, but only the mayoral candidate—the most powerful medium—and the second most powerful are publicly known," Serena explained, her eyes forlorn and flickering with hollow, fearful energy. "Guru Bernie ranks all of the mediums. Only he knows who is next in line. The list isn't publicized for fear of hurting people's feelings."

Snowflakes. "So we ask Bernie?"

"*Guru* Bernie," Serena said sharply, "is unlikely to tell us. Like I said, he has not been himself lately. That's the primary reason I took the steps that I did."

We do keep coming back to that, don't we?

"The levels!" Jason interjected. "Mediums are ranked from Level I to III, with III being the most powerful. It allows the mediums to charge different amounts to customers and lets customers know who's more adept and worth the money."

"Like high-end hairdressers?" I asked, confused.

"I wouldn't know," Serena responded with a toss of her honeyed locks.

"Level III is super expensive, level II less so, and level I is the cheapest. To do readings for the public, you have to be certified on a level." He looked at Serena. "We could get a list of all the public level threes, right?"

She nodded.

"You people have the weirdest rules, I swear," I muttered, frustrated. "The way I see it, there are two possibilities here—well, at least two if we assume Serena is not at the bottom of whatever this conspiracy is. The first is that the next person on the list will have their house burned down. Likely tonight."

"Or the next in succession will *not* have their

home burned down because it's their intent to be the next mayor," Serena said with a pained look. She looked back and forth between Jason and me. "Is this my fault? Did my recall petition cause all this? The ghosts, the fires...Is this really because I did something that gave terrible people an opportunity to manipulate our town?"

It was a good question.

I didn't know the answer yet.

But I was getting closer.

ONCE WE FINISHED OUR CONVERSATION, we walked toward Guru Bernie's town-center cottage to catch up with Emma and Mayor Thornton.

I followed slightly behind Jason and Serena to watch the reactions of those they passed—just in case someone did anything suspicious. No one knew who Jason was in his furry Chewbacca suit, but Serena was well known and clearly identifiable.

And, of course, *possibly* in the middle of all this.

Serena Bliss stated multiple times she started the recall petition due to her issue with Guru

Bernie. She was adamant she only proceeded because she thought the mayor was failing to do enough to handle the town's problems—the ghosts' disappearance being one of those.

Serena was the last to act, following the guru's change and the ghosts' disappearance. That showed a clear timeline: the petition began shortly after these other odd happenings. If the ghosts' disappearance was part of the same plot, this was only neatly tied up in a bow if the homes burning down correlated with Guru Bernie's change.

But it was a chicken and egg situation.

I mean, it seemed like the ghosts were taken out of the equation precisely so this little plot could unfold with no one being the wiser.

Serena tried to recall the mayor after the ghosts vanished and the guru changed. The timing suggested Serena Bliss was in on the conspiracy. Not only aware of it but possibly a participant. That was logical.

Easy.

Clear.

Kind of obvious.

As I followed her and Jason, I had to admit that I didn't find her dishonest. The simple, clear, and obvious explanation just felt...off.

I thought she was cold, arrogant, and perhaps a bit too self-assured.

But I also sensed she adored this town and the people in it. She seemed shaken by the changes, not to mention her mother's sudden departure.

It must have felt like an actual death to Serena.

The death of a loved one wasn't the same for a medium as it was for us. Loved ones who have passed on are usually closer than most people think. For mediums, death just represents a change in the relationship. Not a severing.

With this? Serena was left isolated and alone after her mother vanished, owing to the guru's change and the mayor's distraction.

Would that have made her more susceptible to manipulation?

I didn't know.

And the conflict in the stories I heard from Robert Aurora and the fire men versus just about everyone else was still bothering me.

"Jason!" Melvin Platt ran up to Chewbacca and wrapped his arms around Jason's waist. "You should've told me you were going as Chewbacca! I am totally getting my Obi-Wan costume! Serena!" the boy smiled with excitement. "Can you go as Princess Leia? Huh, can ya?"

Serena stopped walking and smiled at the

excited young man. "Oh, Melvin, I'm sorry, I'm not allowed to go in a secular costume during the Halloween celebration." She leaned down and brushed the hair out of his eyes. "But I think you'll look great as Obi-Wan Kenobi." She raised her eyebrow. "How did you know that Jason was in the Chewbacca costume?"

"I was just over at Aurora Jewelry? Over there?" Melvin turned and pointed to the jewelry store a block away. "There was a man there, and he was talking to someone else, and he was talking about how Jason was here and Jason was in the Chewbacca costume. And then I saw the Chewbacca costume. And I figured it was you. Hey, Jason," Melvin said breathlessly, turning toward him. "Did Ayla come back? Is she here?"

People were talking about Jason in Robert Aurora's shop?

Identifying him. Talking about his costume.

My blood ran cold.

"No, she stayed back in Forkbridge, Mel," Jason's muffled voice told the kid.

"Aw, man, don't call me Mel. My dad calls me Mel when he's mad at me."

Before I could hear whether Serena or Jason thought to ask Melvin who was talking about Jason's costume, a feather touch on my shoulder caused me to turn and shift. I peered through No-Face's mouth in surprise.

"Ms. Arden, I presume." The elderly woman from the town hall meeting, the one with the scar on her face, eyeballed me like the mask's mouth was a peephole in a door. "Remember me?"

I was so unbelievably hot in this costume that my skin was dripping with a small pond's worth of sweat. The whole damn town seemed to know exactly who I was, exactly where I was and could make a beeline for me on a public street.

Great.

They knew where Jason was.

Where I was.

This felt worth it, I thought sarcastically.

"I do remember you, ma'am, but you have me at a disadvantage. I don't know your name." I pulled the mask away from my face and waved the bib-like black cloth hanging off the hard plastic mask. The rush of air was so pleasant I almost passed out from the moment of ecstasy.

"My name is Paula Gauguin," she answered.

"Any relation?" I asked, thinking of the French post-impressionist artist.

"To the painter?" She shook her head. "No. To Bernie Gerald, the current guru of this place? Distantly, yes." Paula leaned in. "He's my cousin."

"I see," I said, even though I didn't. To be honest, I figured this town was so small, half of them had to be related to the other half.

"That's how I know who's on the powerful medium list, in what order people are on it, and how those ranks break down."

I tensed up.

I don't like when people know information they shouldn't.

Not the list. I mean, that was useful, actually.

The thing giving me pause was that this woman found me in a costume designed to hide my identity and then brought up the very thing I'd *just* worked out I probably should take a look at.

"And what makes you think I want to know about that list or anything about who's on it?" I asked her.

"Well, I'm hoping you're as smart as everybody says you are," Paula told me and then knocked on my mask for effect. "Because I'm the third name on that list, and the first two had their houses burned down." She narrowed her eyes. "I like my house, Ms. Arden, and I have no interest in seeing it and all the memories of a lifetime burned to the ground."

This is either the luckiest break I'd gotten so far or the most obvious trap anyone's ever laid for me. "Again, how did you know that I wanted to know who the third name was?" I asked once more.

"I was in the yurt as the three of you discussed the situation," Paula answered, chuckling. "Serena was far more worried about people out on the street, and she assumed the gathering place was empty." She shrugged. "It was not." Her eyes narrowed. "Now, can I count on your help or not?"

CHAPTER SEVENTEEN

The bells attached to the door of Aurora Jewelry rang inside and outside the store as I pulled it open. A wave of images hit me, and I held on tighter to steady myself.

I checked the locked display cases surrounding the entrance to the store, gleaming glass cases filled with engagement and wedding rings, bracelets, earrings. Magical designs were interspersed with regular, normal ones you could find in any jewelry store. My nose wrinkled as a powerful ammonia smell hit my nostrils.

"Hello?" I called out to the empty room.

Who leaves a jewelry store with expensive rubies, diamonds, emeralds, opals, and sapphires unattended and unobserved? It was strange, and that's not even considering there should have been people in the store in the middle of the Halloween festival.

Suddenly, heels clacked across the floor.

"Astra Arden!" Out of the rear of the shop, a petite woman emerged, radiating (what seemed to be) genuine warmth. Her dark brown hair—worn in a way that reminded me of a mysterious hood—nearly covered her bright eyes. "I have heard so much about you, and now you're in my shop. I'm...pleased."

Okay.

Not the greeting I was expecting.

After a brief meeting with Emma, we'd decided the best course of action was to stake out Paula Gauguin's home until nightfall—and beyond—to see who showed up with a can of gasoline and a match. Emma also felt it was finally time to ask Robert Aurora a few questions about the "library" ghost story. She volunteered to guard Jason while I went.

"Why me?" I'd asked her. "You're the cop. Shouldn't you go interview him?"

"You're the witch," Emma responded with a shrug. "You know magical objects, and you know magic and witches. Everything seems to be coalescing around this Robert guy and that necklace around Guru Bernie's neck. It's also a jewelry store." She pointed to my hands. "Grab objects. Let's use everything at our disposal."

And so here I was.

I flexed my fingers. My hands felt odd being exposed to the air, but I'd entered Aurora's Jewelry with my gloves firmly shoved in my back pocket. "I'm sorry, you have me at a disadvantage," I told the woman. "I don't know who you are."

"Jane Aurora," she said, stepping around the display case and extending her hand. I glanced down at it curiously—most people that genuinely had heard of me did not raise their bare hands to shake. "I'm the owner of this establishment."

I took her hand in my own and braced myself for the impact.

Images of Jane and Robert arguing flashed across my mind like polished silver glinting in the sunlight. I must have briefly witnessed ten different fights in the span of a few seconds. Yet, they all appeared to be recent, and Jane seemed to plead with her husband to do something—or not do anything—about whatever they were arguing over.

She let go, and the images mercifully stopped.

"Is it a new piece of jewelry you're looking for,

or are you here to discuss your investigation?" Jane asked, stepping back behind the counter. She pointed toward a case beneath her hand. "I have charming new dolomite pieces that would be perfect for a witch."

I stepped up to the counter, and I positioned my hands against the countertop, bracing slightly just as I had before. Again, just as before, images exploded in my mind.

Edgar burst into the jewelry store and yelled something at Robert Aurora. Robert pointed toward Jane, who was polishing a ring with a rather rude hand gesture. Then with an angry toss of his head, the husband said something to his wife, but I couldn't understand what he was saying. Her face fell with hurt or sadness.

This was so frustrating. The sound was so muffled I could barely make out any of it. I suspected the stones and crystals had absorbed most of the sound waves from the confrontation.

Wait a minute.

I forcefully turned the image in my head.

Edgar.

Edgar carried a gas can.

I pulled my hands from the glass and took a deep breath.

"How do you know I'm a witch?" I asked Jane.

Jane smiled again, her face friendly. "Well, Ms. Arden, I'm not sure if you're aware, but everyone knows you're a witch," she said. "Even though I'm new here, I keep my ear to the ground. Most people are unaware that witches can be more than just environmentally conscious women with a penchant for feminism, but I am. I recognize you."

I nodded and asked, "Through your husband?"

Wow.

That was the wrong thing to say.

Jane's expression grew stormy, but that storm of emotion didn't seem to be directed at me. "If I listened to all the things my husband had to say about the people in this town, I'd believe there was evil around every corner."

I wasn't sure what that meant, but I decided this was as good a time as any to push forward and see what she knew.

"Well, maybe you can help me," I said. Then, leaning in, I claimed, "Someone said they saw Edgar—one of the fire tenders with your husband —with a can of gasoline. He came into the store on some particular day, but the person telling me couldn't remember what day that was." I raised my eyebrow. "You wouldn't happen to remember that day, would you?"

"I do, actually, because it was just a few hours before Mayor Thornton's home burned down, poor woman," Jane told me, her voice ringing with sincerity. "It seemed odd, you know? But, for once, Robert agreed with me, and he told me he would report it to the fire tenders."

"Did he?"

"Well, I assume so," she answered with a nod. "He and his brother Jared left soon after to take care of it."

"His brother *Jared*?" Emma asked for the third time.

"Okay, so let's back up a second," I told her as I balanced on the arm of Paula's sitting room sofa. "Jared and Robert are brothers. Edgar—who has lived here all his life—ran in to talk to Robert, carrying a *gasoline can,* on the night Mayor Thornton's home burned down. I mean, that all seems pretty clear." I tapped my finger against the couch. "Obviously, they burned the mayor's house down. But we're still just dealing with the fires. Not the ghosts."

"Robert's still at the center of that, too, in a way," Emma said. "The captain bought your mother a necklace from his shop, it got lost, and suddenly it's around the neck of the guru." Jason nodded as the detective gestured toward him. "Once Bernie starts wearing the necklace, the ghosts disappear, and he starts acting all whackadoo." Emma thought for a moment. "Something just occurred to me. Can anyone just walk up to the guru and see him? Normally? Like just knock on his door, talk to him?"

Serena shook her head no. "Of course not."

Emma threw her hands in the air. "You say that like I'm supposed to know that. We just walked up and saw him. Knocked on the door, went in. You took us there, in fact."

"The mayor called for your help," Serena explained. "The mayor was housed with the guru, so you went in to see *her*, and because of that, you got to see him. Normally, that wouldn't happen, but it was a special circumstance." She shifted uncomfortably and then sighed. "That, and to be quite honest, I'd hoped you would be able to tell why things are the way they are."

"Who arranges those private meetings?" I asked Serena.

"I do." She sat back with a satisfied expression. "I'm the assistant. I handle those meetings for both the mayor and the guru. Anyone wishing to meet with them must bring their request or grievance to me first."

"You deal with all the problems first? Religious or bureaucratic?" I asked. "Like, every single one of them?"

Serena nodded.

"Jeez, who on earth would want that job?" I burst out without thinking.

Serena made a disapproving face.

"Astra, focus. Serena, had Robert, Jared, or Edgar tried to get a meeting with the guru? Maybe a little more than a month ago?" Emma asked.

Serena sat erect and blinked in surprise. "Yes. In fact, all three had. Jared wanted a meeting to petition for entry into the community. Edgar wanted to talk about expanding the responsibilities of the fire tenders, and Robert—" Serena's eyes darted over toward Jason. "Robert wanted to meet with the guru to discuss removing Mayor Thornton for moral turpitude."

"Moral turpitude?" Emma asked.

"It's an act or behavior that gravely violates the sentiment or accepted standard of the community," Paula explained to the detective.

"Ma'am, I'm a cop. I know what moral turpitude is," Emma told Paula with a bit of an attitude. "What did the mayor do that Bobbo thought was turpitude-ish?"

"That's not a word," I told her.

"Sure it is. I just said it," she responded confidently.

"He was unhappy that the mayor was involved romantically with Captain Harmon," Serena admitted. "Which, to be fair, wasn't an isolated view. Many people were upset about Mayor Thornton's choice of paramours. Myself included."

"I mentioned that uncrossable line, remember?" Jason said, glancing at me.

What did he want, a cookie?

"Do we think it's just these three or the entire fire group?" Serena asked. She looked devastated by the idea that a large portion of the town might be plotting to overthrow the mayor. Which was ironic considering she started the petition.

"I think before we even think about that, we need to get that necklace off of Guru Bernie's neck," I told Serena and then glanced at Emma. "I don't feel all that great about jumping a septuagenarian to do it, though. You?"

"Could I do it? Yes. Do I feel good about it? Not really."

"Couldn't we do what we did to get that note

in Will's pocket? The one Edgar gave him?" Jason asked me.

"We didn't do anything," I told him. "That was Ayla. She can teleport objects and items from one place to another. That's not something I—or anyone else in my family—can do." I looked at my phone. A lot more of the day had passed than I'd thought. "If we leave now, we can get back here with her by sundown. But we have to go now."

"That's cutting it close, especially if Paula's home goes up the same time everyone else's did," Emma said.

Silence fell over the room.

"Okay, let's just do it. I don't want to hurt Guru Bernie. It's the safest course of action," Emma said finally. "No one's been hurt yet. So I'd like to keep it that way if we possibly can."

"Can you stay here?" I asked Serena, glancing at Paula. "I can't leave Jason here. He needs to stay with me."

"You're certainly playing the jealous girlfriend to perfection," Serena popped back at me with an eyebrow raise. "I have no interest in Jason anymore, Ms. Arden. And if you can't trust your boyfriend to stay here alone in the town he grew up in, maybe—"

"Before you dig yourself a hole that's hard to

get out of, why don't you stop right there." Emma turned to Serena. "There's been a threat made on Jason's life,"—Serena and Paula both gasped —"and Astra is the most capable person to guard him against that threat. That's all."

"Says who?" the old woman with the scar asked.

"God," Emma responded without explanation and turned toward the front door, keys in her hand. "Jason's coming with us. End of story."

I TEXTED Ami as soon as my butt hit the Chevy Malibu's front seat to let her know what was going on.

MOM AND AYLA FIGHTING

About what? I texted back.

ATTITUDE

Good or bad attitude, I need Ayla.

WILL TELL MOM

As Emma weaved in and out of traffic on the highway leading to Forkbridge, she wondered aloud, "Do you have any psychic instinct or feeling we're being suckered into a trap? I just...I don't like it. The fire people dudes being involved just makes this so unpredictable."

"I doubt it would be all of them," Jason said from the back. "But it is a hierarchal group, Detective. If the people in charge told them to change how they're supposed to operate, they would do it. They would have to."

"Especially if the fire spirit—" I stopped, shocked I didn't see it before. "I'm such an idiot."

"Yeah, sure, okay," Emma agreed with me. "But why?"

"There are no fire spirits," I told her, smacking my gloved hand on the car seat. "The 'fire spirits' they claim they're talking to are just ghosts. They said the 'fire spirits' wanted the homes to burn down, and that's why they let the fires consume them—but that's impossible. We were at that fire —nothing was talking because there are no ghosts in Cassandra. There's no one telling them that—well, obviously someone is. But it's not a legit spiritual message from the great beyond."

"Robert," Emma said. "That's why he's telling a different story about the ghosts. He's claiming to get information from ghosts he 'checks out'—like the fire spirits—when he's really not. That must be how he's getting them to follow him."

"Maybe that's what Edgar didn't want Will to tell you?" Jason mused.

"Maybe," I said with a shrug. We pulled up in

front of Arden House. "Can you watch him?" I asked Emma, hitching my head toward Jason.

She nodded and pulled out her weapon.

"Be right back." As soon as I stepped on the walkway, Ayla shot out of the front door and glared at me. "Hey. Mom know you're going?" My younger sister shook her head and marched past me, her feet stomping heavily on the ground as she made her way to her car.

"Just go. I'll tell Mom," Ami called from the doorway. "I'm not sure what's going on with her, but she was locked up in your room with Archie pretty much all day." With Archie. My supposed divine assistant in the middle of a star card case? "Your bird is the only one she seems to be able to talk to without exploding."

I looked up, squinting into the trees to see if I could spot the owl, but I saw nothing. "I'll see if I can find out what it's about."

"Did you figure out who did what yet?" Ami asked.

"Maybe," I told her. "It's coming together into a big picture. We seem to have figured out what's going on. But, I still don't understand why."

Ami glanced toward the car. "Jason's still alive. That's good. Oh!" She raced out and handed me a plastic baggie. "Althea made some sodium bicarbonate that will expand and replicate as soon as it hits the fire. It will keep replicating itself until the fire is smothered out. You might need it." I took it. "Thea said you only need a pinch even if the fire is huge. Like a tiny, tiny pinch."

I looked at it. It looked like baking soda, and it was a lot more than a pinch.

Actually, wait...isn't sodium bicarbonate baking soda?

So, enchanted, replicating baking soda.

Cool.

"Tell her thanks. This might come in handy."

"Are we going, or are you and Ami just going to run your mouths all day?" Ayla yelled from the passenger side window. "Come on, the sun's going to go down soon!"

Ami stared at me, a smile plastered on her face. "Have fun."

I shook the baggie, nodded, and turned back to the car.

CHAPTER EIGHTEEN

"I don't know you. Who're you?" Ayla asked Paula Gauguin bluntly, her arms crossed defensively as she confronted the third most powerful psychic in Cassandra, Florida, on the eve of Halloween.

I sighed with exhaustion.

Ayla had remained tense in the car the entire trip from Forkbridge to Cassandra. Her glares into the rearview mirror were the only form of communication I obtained. Oh, I'd tried to engage her, explain the situation in Cassandra, and encourage conversation—but I gave up halfway across the lake bridge.

Before I could warn Paula, the older lady stood up from her recliner and towered over

Ayla, staring down at her with something vaguely threatening in her eyes. "Young lady, you're in *my* home. Mine. It may burn down tonight, but for the moment, this is my castle."

"That doesn't tell me who you—"

"And while I appreciate that you've all come to help me," Paula continued, barreling through Ayla's interruption, "that doesn't give you any right to speak rudely—and certainly not to me, in my own home. So if you plan to hold on to that attitude, you can just turn right back around and go." She raised her eyebrow. "I don't need anyone's help that much."

Ayla glared indignantly at the woman.

After five seconds of silent scrutiny from the thirteen-year-old, Paula turned and scanned a bookshelf to the right, grabbing a light green hardcover and holding it out to Ayla. My youngest sister reached from under her crossed arms and carefully took the book. When she tilted it up, she—and I—could see the title.

Miss Manners' Guide to Excruciatingly Correct Behavior

Oh, snap, Ms. Gauguin.

"I never assume people know what they don't seem to know, and I'd rather inform than chastise," Paula told Ayla, her voice no less stern.

"Now, I've heard a lot about you from some of the ghosts that *used* to call this place home, Miss Ayla." Paula tilted her head. "None of them told me you were a spoiled brat."

"I'm not a spoiled brat!" she responded hotly, her cheeks burning with embarrassment. "I just have to take up for myself! If I don't, no one else is going to!"

"Is that so?" Paula looked across the room at Ayla. "You don't know me, Little Miss. I haven't done anything but allowed you into my home. Of course, when I stomp on your dreams, you have my permission to get your back up—within reason—but until *then*, I will expect the respect every being is due from any other being on this planet. Especially in my own space. Do we understand each other?"

Emma, Jason, Serena, and I stood there silently, watching the exchange.

With all of the training I've had over the years, you'd think I'd have had at least one class on how to deal with an irate adolescent. However, the ministry did not believe it was necessary to teach us how to deal with angry teenagers.

"If I had to guess, they'd come right at sunset," Paula said, glancing out the window at the vibrant sky. "I'm supposed to be at the town square doing a group reading then." Paula squinted out the window. "Is that an owl in my tree?"

Emma turned. "Did Archie follow us?" she asked, pointing out the window.

When I turned around, there was the goddess's own owl perched in a tree outside Paula's window, keeping a close eye on Ayla. "Let me go find out what he's doing," I told Emma, glancing at Jason. "Watch him?"

"I feel like a dog let off the leash at a dog park," Jason mumbled to Serena. "They think they have their freedom, but they don't, not really. The leash is just the watchful eye of the owner making sure they never get too far away."

"Did you have too much wine at lunch?" I heard Emma ask as I walked into Paula's backyard.

"Hey," I called quietly. Even though the fence surrounding Paula's backyard was tall, it didn't prevent someone from spying on us from one of the nearby houses. "Nice of you to actually show up here."

"If I clock your tone, you believe I haven't been working on the star card case," Archie yelled from atop an oak tree, where he was hiding. His head tilted, and he moved it in a circle in that creepy way owls have. Then he blinked. "You don't really know what I've been doing all day, do you?" I opened my mouth to answer, but before I could speak, he added, "No. No, you don't."

"Oh my Hades, is everyone going to pull an attitude today?" I muttered under my breath as I combed my hair with my fingers. "No, I have no idea. That's why I came out to see you. To find out what you've been up to, what you know, and what you don't."

"This house is going to burn down tonight," Archie told me. He looked proud—as if he was telling me something I couldn't possibly know.

"I know." Archie made a *humph* sound. "We're here to save the house tonight, dude. Sorry to spoil your big reveal, if it was one. So how did you know?"

Archie blinked and shifted his head a few times. "How did I know what?" He spread his wings and flapped them once without moving.

"Why did you say that this house is going to burn down tonight? How did you know that?" I inquired politely. He harrumphed once more and began preening his immaculately clean and perfectly arranged feathers. "Archie?"

The goddess's own owl went on preening.

This bird was dancing a jig on my last nerve.

"Archie!"

"Your mother and Ami collaborated with the oracles to see if they could make any headway on what was going on in Cassandra," Archie explained with a shrug. "They did and arrived at the same conclusion and location you did—here." He waved his wing in the air. "They did it from the comfort of their own home, of course, without putting themselves in any danger or even venturing outside the protection wards."

I stared at him.

"And they did it quickly enough for Althea to research, find, and create the recipe for fire powder Ami gave you," Archie added smugly.

I pulled out my phone and texted Ami.

You guys solved the case there?

ARCHIE WASN'T SUPPOSED TO TELL YOU

Well, he did. Why didn't you say anything?

MOM DIDN'T WANT YOU TO FEEL LIKE YOU WASTED YOUR TIME

I breathed in once and breathed out slowly. *What is it you know? Shouldn't we meet and compare notes?*

ORACLES SAY YOU KNOW EVERYTHING WE DO. ALL GOOD. GOOD LUCK.

I stared at my phone.

"You know, I *am* the goddess's own owl," Archie said, looking down at me. "You were given magic by Athena, but you hardly ever use it. Yes, I'm here to assist you in your endeavors. But I'm also here to ensure that Athena's wishes are carried out. Sometimes, that involves more than just you."

This again. The *nosy-goddess-in-the-sky* watching over a couple of small towns in Florida stuff. "Okay, I'll bite. And what exactly does Athena want?" I asked him, my brow furrowed. "Tell me. I'd love to know."

"Oh, please. What does it matter?" Archie shot back petulantly. "You don't believe there's a goddess or an Athena or that she cares one whit about you. Or anybody else. Why should I tell you what she wants? You don't even believe she exists."

"But I haven't since we started this, Archie," I said sincerely, confused at the bird's sudden attitude switch. "You told me you didn't care, that my belief didn't matter. So why is it suddenly a problem now?"

Archie looked away.

"You know something," I observed.

He refused to look back.

"Something you're not telling me," I added.

Archie's head snapped back, and his feathers puffed up. "Astra, the things I know but won't tell you span thousands of years. The Library of Alexandria held only a fraction of the knowledge contained within my adorable featherhead."

I rolled my eyes skyward. "You know, I spent years working for people with an agenda that they never bothered to tell me about, Archie. I didn't like it then." I pointed my finger at him. "I don't like it now."

"You don't know what you don't know because you don't *want* to know what you don't know," the bird responded with a final flap of his wings. "Please forgive me if I become irritated. I honestly didn't expect you to be as dimwitted as you are about some things."

With that last zinger delivered, he launched himself into the blue sky, disappearing behind the house.

"DON'T SLAM THAT DOOR!" Paula called as I slammed the back door.

"What's with you?" Emma asked, surprised.

"Everyone is mad at me," I grumbled. "Ayla barely speaks to me, and now the damn bird is giving me attitude because I don't know what I don't know, and he thinks I should know what I don't know."

Emma gave me a wide-eyed look and shook her head. "I...he...what?"

"We have to stop now," Ayla warned us, her voice tense. "Shut off the lights. Shut them off and hide! Now!"

We all looked at Ayla, but nobody moved.

Ayla had two powers I knew of. One? She could teleport things. Big things, little things, live things, inanimate things. Two? She could talk to ghosts. She could call them, she could see them, she could sense them—

Wait a minute.

I snapped my head and looked at her.

She could *sense* them.

"You sense ghosts coming this way," I guessed. "Ghosts with some type of malevolent intent."

"Angry ghosts, and tons of them. Like, *tons* of them," she whispered. "They're headed straight here right now. Turn off all the lights! Now, hurry! And get the rock out! Now!"

We all dove for whatever light or lamp was near and darkened the entire house within seconds. Once that was done, we ran away from the front windows. I pulled the crystal Archie had given me from my pocket. "Ayla, there's only one. How is one rock supposed to protect everybody?"

"One rock isn't, duh," she said as she raced toward me and snatched it out of my hand. "Get behind me, everybody. And grab me somewhere. Like, just make sure you're touching me. Ow! Don't *pinch* me! Just make contact. Oh my gosh," she said with exasperation.

Like a gigantic game of vertical Twister, everyone shuffled and moved and made way so we could all huddle up behind Ayla.

"I think we're all chained up here, Ayla," I told her.

"Thank you," Ayla whispered, glancing at me.

I turned to her, surprised. "For what?"

"For trusting me."

A knock on the front door brought that conversation to an abrupt halt.

"Do I answer it?" Paula whispered.

"No," Ayla told her. "Stay here. If it's them, I'll make it so they can't see us."

"You'll do what?" I asked, alarmed. "Ayla, what are you—"

"*Trust* me, Astra," she responded, her face serious, her eyes intense with concentration. "I know what I'm doing."

I wished that *I* knew what she was doing, but there was no time to ask.

A key turned in a lock.

The front door slowly creaked open.

"No one talk, no one break connection to me," Ayla whispered, and she closed her eyes.

I heard it before I felt it.

It began as a trickle of water, then became a steady stream, and finally a waterfall. My skin felt icy, as if I'd been wrapped in an invisible gel that cooled the air around me by several degrees. Everything in Paula's house was tinted blue as if illuminated by a dispersed light that came from nowhere but was everywhere.

Guru Bernie walked into the living room and looked around. He was followed by Edgar and then Jared Upton. Jinny, Madame Margo's assistant, brought up the rear holding the key. They listened quietly, their gaze passing over the six of us hiding in the corner behind a chair as if we didn't exist.

Robert Aurora was not with them.

Finally, Guru Bernie nodded. "We're good."

"You're sure she's not here?" Edgar asked Jinny. He didn't speak at an ear-splitting level the way he had before. "Maybe you should go upstairs and make sure she's not taking a nap. Death would bring the state authorities in."

"I know the schedule, but sure, I'll double-check." Jinny nodded and ran up the stairs.

"This is the last one we need to do," Guru Bernie told Jared and Edgar with a shrug. "Once this one's out of the way, we recall Mayor Moron, let everyone know the fire spirits healed your hearing even as they burned down the other homes, and that you are the new chosen one." Edgar nodded, his shoulders back as if ready to accept a medal. "We'll elect you as mayor and replace that sanctimonious assistant Serena with Jinny."

Serena tensed at the statement.

"That should solve everything," Jared Upton said with a nod.

"Men in charge of Cassandra, finally, assisted by a woman that knows her place," Edgar said with a paternalistic sanctimony that made my hands twitch. "No more women flagrantly disregarding the rules of the community, no more shrewish whining in town meetings, no more stupid ideas about banning gasoline. No more guru talking about peace and love like some pansy."

Well. *That* was offensive.

"We have the ghosts under control," Guru Bernie nodded. "Next, we get the women. Finally, any men that refuse to follow the new way of doing things."

"What about those witches from the next town?" Edgar asked.

"What about them?" Guru Bernie laughed. "What are *they* gonna do?"

"Don't let go," Ayla whispered.

The three men's eyes widened as Ayla lifted her hands. One hand still clutched her ghost rock. The other palmed out toward the guru.

"What was that?" Guru Bernie asked. He looked around, and then cursed with surprising gusto. "I swear I heard something."

"Did you? I thought it was the wind," Edgar said, looking around.

"Why don't you use those new ears I gave you and listen harder?" Bernie hissed back at him. "I'm telling you, I heard something."

Emma and I gripped Ayla's shoulders tightly as she tensed, made a few motions, and whispered something I couldn't understand. The hexagon necklace vanished from Guru Bernie's neck in the blink of an eye. The old man collapsed to the ground as if struck by an unseen punch.

My thirteen-year-old sister brought the necklace and rock together with her hands straight in front of her. I felt a dizzying, wrenching sensation of the world lurching rightward. Then a blazing wave of energy washed over me.

"No!" Jared shouted. He stared at us, his eyes wild. "What have you done!"

"Stopped you," Ayla remarked, shrugging her shoulders. "Ugh." She suddenly became unsteady on her feet, and I caught her before she fell to the ground. "I'm afraid I'm going to throw up, Astra." She raised her eyes to me, looking frightened. "If I do, I'm really sorry."

"I gotcha, kid," I told her. Ayla looked suddenly frail, frightened, and like the child she was under all that bravado. "You did your part. I got it from here."

She smiled weakly at me and sank into my arms, clutching me close.

"Mabel! Evangeline! Deodat!" Paula shouted, her head swiveling on her neck like she was watching a dozen ping pong matches all at once. "You're here. You're back! Oh, my stars, I missed you so much!"

Edgar's eyes grew wide, and he ran toward the front door.

"Mom!" Serena cried and then sobbed with relief, staring at the empty space in front of her. "Where have you been? Are you all right?"

I could feel the reunions happening all around me, even if I couldn't see it. Cries of joy slowly trickled in from the street.

"Could I get maybe some help down here if you're all not too busy, maybe?" a rough, kindly voice asked. "I'm an old man and not as spry as I used to be."

Emma approached Guru Bernie with caution and helped the elderly man up. His face was lined with joy, his watery eyes gleaming with delight— a completely different expression than the man I'd met a day ago. "Thank you. I feel like I haven't seen the light in a month."

"Okay, I have to admit, I don't understand," I said, frowning. "Was he possessed by an angry ghost? Is that what it was?"

"You know what Psychíkinesis is, Astra?" Guru Bernie asked me.

I gasped, and my body went cold. "Soul bending. Psychíkinesis is the power to manipulate souls." Soul bending was nasty, nasty stuff. A witch power that was, thankfully, exceedingly rare.

The old man nodded. "Robert Aurora is a

witch, Astra," Guru Bernie told me. "He and his brother"—Bernie glanced at Jared Upton with a sad look on his face—"can manipulate the souls of the living and the dead. They came here to take over Cassandra. Use it for their own purposes." Again, a sympathetic, sad gaze cast at Jared. "I could see it all in Robert's mind."

"Well, you weren't using it!" Jared barked angrily as he struggled in Jason's two-armed grasp. "Love and peace? Come on, I mean, come on! This isn't the 1960s, old man! You live in a town full of ghosts and mediums, and you throw festivals and serve cocktails with cutesy names? You people are—"

"Not yours to manipulate," I told him angrily, my arms still wrapped around Ayla. "Guru Bernie, what do you mean you saw it in Robert's mind?"

"He used me, dear. Lived in my body, walked around like my skin was a costume he could put on and take off." Guru Bernie coughed once, then again, and frowned. "Oh, my, cigarettes are terrible things." Paula handed the guru a peppermint. "Thank you, dear Paula. Terrible things. In any case, your sister threw him out of me. Evicted him. She's quite a pip, that one." He smiled proudly at Ayla, and she smiled back.

"How did he get...um, in you?" Emma asked.

"Through the necklace," Bernie answered, pointing. "I bless all jewelry, you know. One of my great pleasures," he said, smiling happily. "I found the necklace on the bathroom counter in my bungalow. I knew it had to be Serena's or Lillian's, so I picked it up. Then everything went black."

"My mother says Guru Bernie began calling the ghosts to him about a month ago. Though I guess it wasn't Guru Bernie," Serena explained as she looked back and forth between us and empty space. "Each one that visited him disappeared. Many, she believes, were captured in the stone. She was. But not all were there." She smiled briefly. "Those that realized so many were disappearing without explanation scattered and ran away. They were afraid of what was happening."

"And you all did this because you're misogynists?" I asked Jared.

He shrugged. "Good a reason as any. That, and boredom." Jared glared at me. "I *like* power. I was good at it in Paranormopolis. So was my brother."

"Well, at least he's honest," Emma pointed out.

Power-hungry people. Half the time, they

didn't believe their own bull. They just used whatever excuse they could for control. The bull made it palatable to others. Maybe even to themselves.

"We have to find Robert," I said with some concern. "Who knows what he's doing now. And Edgar—"

I heard it before I saw it.

Choking.

Jason choking.

I slid Ayla into a chair and turned to see Jason's face red and sweat on his brow. Jared's lips twitched with an evil smile.

"Let him go!" I said. Jason let go of Jared, no longer able to hold him while his oxygen was cut off by an invisible force. I snatched Jared before he could flee the room. "I was talking to *you*, moron." I yanked him by the shirt and threw him up against the wall. "Quit manipulating Jason! Let him go!"

Jason's hands were clutching his throat, and the color was draining from his face. Serena flew from across the room, but he was choking on nothing other than an evil man's soul magic. She could do nothing to help, and her face twisted in frightened frustration.

Starlight glowed in my hands, and my fingers

sparked with tiny angry lightning bolts. "Jared, so help me—let him go!"

Jason ripped open his collar, his lips turning blue.

Slamming Jared against a wall had no effect. Demanding that he stop had no effect. The evil witch gave me a bemused look as if he'd already gotten the better of me. Like I'd already failed.

Think, Astra.

Think.

I looked down at the white light in my hands.

"In the name of Athena, in the name of Astraea, I take your power from you!" I shouted angrily, my sizzling white-hot hands reaching for his throat. "You have abused it, abused it to hurt people! You won't hurt anyone else!" I felt a pop, like a champagne bottle being uncorked, and heard a gasp behind me.

Jason began coughing violently and inhaling sharply, loudly.

That was good.

That meant air.

Jared Upton's eyes widened as he laughed sarcastically. The laugh faded as a horrified expression crept across his face. He crumpled to Paula's beige Berber carpet and lay still, turning white.

"Thank you, Astra," Jason huffed.

I nodded, still staring at Jared.

"Judge, jury, and executioner?" Emma mumbled, her eyes wide. "That's not scary at all, Arden. Nope. I'm not creeped out by what I just saw one iota."

"Relax. He's not dead," I told her.

I leaned down and looked over the collapsed man lying in a heap.

At least, I didn't *think* he was dead.

CHAPTER NINETEEN

"*The* ghosts didn't mean to kill them," Ayla told me. "It just happened."

Emma tapped her purple nitrile-gloved hand against Robert Aurora's waxy white skin. "If I hadn't seen it with my own eyes, I wouldn't have believed it," she said, looking up. "But my dude is solidly frozen. As if he was abandoned on the summit of Mt. Everest without a coat." She cast a glance at Edgar, who was leaning against the wall, a startled expression on his face. "That one as well."

Jared Upton was not dead after my super-zap, but Robert Aurora and Edgar?

They *definitely* were.

After the confrontation, Emma'd immediately

called the captain. He and the mayor joined us at Paula's, and after assessing the situation, Captain Harmon arranged for a cruiser to transport Jared and Jinny to Forkbridge jail. Then, as a group, we set out in search of Robert Aurora.

The search didn't take long. We found him—and Edgar—frozen solid in the chilly back stockroom of Aurora Jewelry.

"What do you mean, the ghosts didn't mean to kill them?" I asked Ayla.

Ayla cast a sidelong glance, nodded, paused, and then nodded again. "Gertrude says the ghosts knew what happened and who had captured them, and they were all super angry," she said, turning back to me. "When they found Robert, they all crowded in around him, yelling, and it quickly became frigid in here. Like, crazy fast." Ayla cast a glance at Robert. "I guess it got too cold for them to live."

I nodded and looked at Emma. "That makes sense. When a ghost is in a room, the temperature can start to decrease. A single ghost can get the temperature down to almost freezing in a few minutes," I explained. "But only in spots, so it's a localized thing."

"Yeah. Mostly," Ayla said. "But some ghosts can drop temperatures even further. *Below* freezing, even. And the more ghosts that are in one place, the further the temperature can drop. And if they're *stacked*, if they dual-occupy space," she explained, "they can cause a flash-freezing event. So everything in *their* space gets whammied with cryogenic-level temperatures."

"And they didn't mean to do this, huh?" Captain Harmon asked suspiciously.

"Oh, Dan, what would it matter if they did?" Mayor Thornton asked him. "Are you going to arrest all our ghosts on suspicion of retaliatory murder?" She paused and looked at him, but he didn't answer. "Would it matter, really matter, to anyone if you just let it go?"

Captain Harmon stared at the two frozen mediums. "I imagine Jared Upton is going to want to know who killed his brother."

"Jared Upton's a witch," I told Captain Harmon. "He'll know as soon as he hears how the body was found. No one will need to tell him." I examined the two men. "Call their deaths a cryogenic treatment accident or something, and call it a day. There's one three doors down. Heck, arrest Jared for it. What's he going to do? Explain what really happened?" I chuckled. "They'll stick him in the loony bin."

I heard a sigh escape from the captain. "Okay,

Arden, let's rein it in a little bit," Captain Harmon told me fiercely. "I'd like to keep the police department from becoming completely and totally corrupt on my watch."

"It's not corruption; it's just…creative disposal of a problem."

He glared at me, and his eyes flashed with impatience. Emma rolled her eyes.

Mayor Thornton told her boyfriend, "You can leave them here. We'll call the state police, and they'll have another strange story to tell their friends about Cassandra. Nobody is going to look any further into anything." The self-assured mayor's voice was smooth and persuasive as she decreed what would happen next. "They never do, they never will, and they certainly will not this time."

I cast a glance toward the store's entrance. Guru Bernie was huddled with Jane Aurora just past the archway. Jason and Serena stood guard over the two as the town's spiritual leader consoled the recently widowed woman. She looked sad but also…relieved.

"Is she a witch?" Emma asked, following my eyes.

"I don't know. Maybe. Probably." It shouldn't matter. It shouldn't matter to anyone what she is as long as she's a decent person—and nothing indicated Jane Aurora had anything to do with what her husband had done.

"What happens to her now?" Emma asked me. "If she is, I mean."

"Maybe that's what they're talking about," I said with a shrug.

I DIDN'T HAVE to deal with any police paperwork, so I left Aurora Jewelry with Ayla and took her to the Piggy Pickle Shack. We ordered two plates of brisket with potato salad and fried okra, took our plates to a booth in the back, and sat down.

I sipped my sweet tea. "Exciting day."

"Yeah," Ayla replied. She took a bite of the brisket after picking it up with her fingers. As my sister chewed, her gaze was drawn to the table. Swallowing, she replaced the meat on the butcher paper and turned to face the restaurant's front. Ayla's attention focused on the revelry and raucousness just beyond the window.

"Not hungry?" I asked her.

"What?" she asked, turning back. "Oh. Yeah. No. I don't know."

"You were incredible today, Ayla."

She shrugged, and her eyes dropped back to the table.

I leaned forward. "Look at me."

Ayla hesitantly raised her eyes.

"You were incredible today. I know soldiers in the military that might not have handled themselves as well as you did. No lie." She stared back at me, expressionless. I'd thought my comment would get at least a half-smile from her, but nothing. Not so much as a blink.

"I know," she answered, sounding exhausted. "Archie said Athena said I would do really good if I just knew what to do." Her cheeks were colorless, and all the fight and attitude seemed to have drained out of her. "I just wish someone in my family would believe that." She frowned. "I had to be taught by a *bird*."

"Ayla, I have no idea what it is you did, if you want to know the truth." Her eyes widened. "I couldn't have taught you that. Between you, me, and the wall—and if you ever tell Mom I said this, I will deny it left, right, and sideways—I don't know that Mom could have taught you how to do what you did, either."

"Really?" she asked, perking up.

"Ayla Arden, you took on a *soul bender*—and an evil, mean, jerk one at that. You broke hundreds of ghosts out of a soul bender prison—"

"It was more like almost a *thousand*, really," she interrupted, her cheeks pinking up with pride. "I mean, it was a lot. I know what Mom said about honeycombs and all, but there must have been a *lot* of honeycombs in that thing." Suddenly, she paled. "You're not...you're not mad that your owl was with me the whole time you were working?"

I paused for a moment and ate more brisket. It gave me time to formulate an answer—because I wasn't sure what that answer would be.

Initially, I'd been annoyed at Archie's disappearing act, especially once the case became a star card case. The bird had been almost no help. No information, barely any suggestions. The most he gave me this past week was shovels full of attitude about what a know-it-all he was and what an idiot I was.

But I'd saved Jason, even without his help. To do it, I just had to be in the right place at the right time. That's all.

Well, okay, that and shoot lightning bolts from my fingers that meticulously stripped away another witch's inherent power...

Huh.

Emma was right.

That *was* kind of creepy, now that I thought about it.

"None of us knew what to do to help the town, Ayla," I began quietly. "Or the ghostly townsfolk that had been imprisoned. I might have been able to get the necklace on my own, but I would have just brought it to Mom. *And* I might have hurt poor Guru Bernie in the process," I admitted regretfully. "So, no. Not mad. Archie gave you the tools and the information to put things right here. I'm quite sure I couldn't have done that on my own. At least not today, not before Halloween."

"Or without the goddess," Ayla tossed back at me, her eyes sparkling.

I took another drink. "Let's not push it."

Ayla's eyes were intense and searching. "I heard you, though. You asked Athena for help. And Astraea. You did what you did in their name, and it worked."

I looked down at my gloved hands and flexed my fingers. "I suppose. I couldn't think of anything else to do." I tilted my head. "Part of me doesn't know why I said that, if you want to know the truth."

Almost gleeful, Ayla leaned closer. "That's because when you're completely trapped and there's no way out, when you don't know what to do? Truth pops up, and today it popped out of your mouth." She frowned. "That's how it works for me, anyway." She paused and frowned even more deeply. "I probably need to work on that. Sometimes truth should stay in my mouth."

"Sometimes your truth is communicated in a way that makes it hard to process, Ayla. I'll admit that." I checked my phone. "Looks like Emma's done with all the paperwork and body pickup and whatnot." I looked up. "Why don't you finish so we can head home?"

Crestfallen, Ayla peered out the window at the street with palpable longing. Then she turned and picked at her plate.

"Wow, Ayla, you did great!" Althea hugged Ayla to her chest and kissed her on the top of the head. "I'm a little bummed you didn't use the fire powder, but, I mean, since the lady's house didn't burn down, that's probably good. Heh. The Arden sisters are bad a—"

"Language," Aunt Gwennie warned.

Mom nodded. "But I agree. Ayla, you were really the star of the show today. Young lady, very well done. What an incredible story." My mother then peered at Ayla over her reading glasses. "You did your coven quite proud."

"She did her family quite proud," I corrected.

Mom looked at me sharply.

"What?" I asked with exasperation. "We're a family first. I'm sorry if that bothers you, but we are." Ayla shifted her gaze between my mother and me, her face tense. "Speaking of that, I'd like to take my sisters to the Halloween festival tomorrow. Guru Bernie mentioned that he has an announcement he wants us to hear." Again, I looked at my mother. "Any problem with that, Ma?"

The "Ma" hit her like fingernails on a chalkboard.

Maybe I should have approached that differently.

Seeing Ayla's face light up with excitement, though, supercharged me, and I didn't back up or bow and scrape in apology.

"Ayla's too young—"

"Ayla *saved* the ghosts, and they're kind of the town guardians. So no ghost in Cassandra is going to let anyone harm a hair on Ayla's head. Or any of ours, really."

The high priestess of Athena frowned. "I'd really prefer that you didn't—"

"Well, I mean, *I'm* an adult," Ami said cautiously, wading into the fray. "And I'd like to go. We've heard so much about their Halloween celebration. I'd like to see it."

I glanced toward Aunt Gwennie and found her attention solely focused on her knitting. My aunt could be a sagacious woman.

"I'm not technically an adult," Althea jumped in, "but close enough to it that if you say no, I'll *probably* slip out and go anyway." She shrugged with a nonchalance I envied. "I've heard about the festivals. If I get grounded, it would totally be worth it. You can't come and get me, anyway. You're not allowed in the town." A look of anger flashed across my mother's face. "So, yeah. I'm in."

"And I would help her sneak out," Ami admitted. Althea raised her eyebrow. "Not that you need any help. I mean, I just would. If you did." Althea continued staring. "Which you don't."

We all turned toward Ayla, who was biting her lip.

"Do you want to join this mutiny, Ayla Arden?" my mother asked, her voice slightly sharper. Mom glanced at me briefly as if to blame me for all this.

Which, you know, was fair.

Just saying.

Slowly, Ayla shook her head no.

Mom looked at Ayla with surprise and confusion in the shadows of her eyes. "You don't want to go to Cassandra with your sisters, Ayla? Why not?"

"I *do* want to go," my sister answered, measuring her words carefully. "I want to go more than anything. But you already said I can't go, and asking again would just be hounding you." Ayla took a deep breath. "I was scared today. I mean, like, really scared. Pee in my pants scared."

"Oh, sweetheart," Aunt Gwennie murmured, putting down her knitting.

"But Astra was there," she said and briefly smiled at me. "And even though I was mean to her and mad at her and everything, she protected me." Ayla frowned. "Well, nothing attacked *me*, really, but I felt like it could happen. And I knew Astra would stop it, the same way she stopped Jared from killing Jason."

Althea nodded. "Always, sis. We're always there for each other."

Ayla nodded back. "But, like, if I treat everyone bad and push them away and don't listen, then maybe someday I'll find *myself* alone even though I need somebody. And you won't be there for me because I *made* you not be there." She breathed out loudly. "That's scary. And I don't want that. I don't want to be alone."

My mother looked at Ayla as if she'd never quite seen her before.

"Perhaps you are at last approaching the truths that matter," Mom said finally. Her voice was quiet, yet with a steely tone. "The goddess always has you, child. You'll never be truly alone." Mom paused then and looked back at me. "You may go to the festival with your sisters."

"Wait, what?!" Ayla screeched.

"If the goddess trusts you to do what you did today, surely I can trust you to behave for one night in Cassandra," Mom said.

I rolled my eyes.

If I'd known Mom would let Ayla off her leash because an invisible person in the sky decided she could be trusted, I would have faked a holy revelation months ago.

"They're all growing up, Minnie," Aunt Gwennie told my mother affectionately.

"Yes," Mom admitted and then glanced over each one of us. "May the goddess Athena help anyone who crosses these four."

CHAPTER TWENTY

"She looks like she belongs here," Jason commented, watching Ayla and Melvin marvel over a street painter painting *aural art*, a portrait of visitors that included depictions of their aura (as related to the medium artist by a ghost). My younger sister's eyes were alight with a top-of-the-world elation.

"She does," I admitted with a nod. "I imagine she feels a kinship with your people and their interconnectedness with the ghosts. My mother's been a little controlling with her in that regard."

And so many other regards, but not the time and the place.

"My people. My people," Jason murmured and then leaned against the brick wall behind him for support. He looked out over the street filled with booths, visitors, cheer, and merriment and whispered, "I will put a division between my people and thy people."

"Did you just quote the bible?" I asked, a little astonished.

"Maybe," he said, his voice strong and his expression a half-smile.

"You must try this fried butter," Emma said as she returned with Ami and Althea. She dashed ahead of me and shoved a crisp, fried square in my face. "I never imagined something could taste so good."

"That's the single most unhealthy food I've ever heard of." I pushed her hand and the fried monstrosity away. "I'm not eating that."

"No, this might be," Ami held up half of a gooey, fried thing.

"Ugh, what is that?"

Althea held up the other half. "Fried Snickers Bar."

My stomach churned at the thought.

"It's sundown," Jason announced, smiling. He pushed himself off the wall and watched the crowd. As if in a queue, the crush of people on the closed street moved to the east toward the park.

"Come on. Guru Bernie's going to address the crowd."

"Is this what he wanted us to hear?" I asked.

"I suspect so. Maybe," Jason said, shrugging. "Maybe not. Either way, you should really see this. It's a heck of a thing."

I tapped Ayla on the shoulder as the quickening flow of people took us to her, and she whirled, smiling. "What's up? Melvin and I were—"

"I know, we could see you. We're all going toward the park for Bernie's address. You guys need to stay with us, okay?"

She nodded excitedly, grabbed Melvin, and pulled him toward us.

THE CRUSH of people ebbed and flowed around us. The park was filled with people, a temporarily erected stage set up for concerts on one side. There was a lot of activity with crew members placing long switches near the microphone. Typically, crowds of this size got louder, but this one seemed to grow quieter as everyone moved closer to the stage. Respectful whispers traveled between the breeze while we waited.

Not everyone had shown up. I could hear the partying continuing along the closed main thoroughfare behind me, a party just as loud and raucous as before. People were quiet in the park, on the other hand. Serious.

For all the seriousness, though, the atmosphere was electric.

"This is my favorite part," a woman in front of me whispered to her husband.

"I never *see* anything," he told her. "Frankly, I think you're all imagining it."

"Oh, Charles," the woman sighed, wrapping her arms around him. She looked up with a smile. "That's because you don't really believe. You just have to have faith. Just try it. Believe you'll see them. I promise you, you will."

Charles didn't answer.

The crowd fell silent as Guru Bernie emerged from the shadows at the stage's side. He moved gracefully toward the microphone, dressed in a long flowing white robe. Serena and Mayor Thornton trailed behind him.

"Good evening, the people!" Bernie said jovially. "Now, before we get started, remember just down here?" Bernie pointed down in front of the stage. "There are a lot of candles. So be careful where you walk, yeah? We don't want anyone getting hurt. Okay? Okay? Okay." He looked off stage. "Let's turn the lights off."

"What?" I asked, alarmed. I'd been trained in crowd control. Unfortunately, plunging a crowd of drunks into complete darkness wasn't one of the safety options.

"I promise you, it will be fine," Jason told me. He reached out and grabbed my gloved hand. "Just don't anyone walk around, okay?"

I grabbed Ayla's hand.

The park plunged into darkness.

"So, years ago, our ancestors realized that sometimes, the truth was closer. Yeah? Yeah?" Guru Bernie smiled cheerfully, his face illuminated by an eerie candle glow. "They said the veil is thin. The veil is thin. Tonight, the veil is thin! The most thin it's going to be for another year! Just tonight. But what is this cockamamie veil they're talking about?"

The crowd laughed softly.

"The veil is where we bump right up against eternity," Bernie said, his voice firm. "It's the thing that separates us from everyone that came before. Where the seen—what we are, yeah? Meets the unseen. The ghosts," he whispered. "The eternal truths. God. They're all just beyond that veil. Right there!"

The crowd stood in front of the stage, watching Bernie with rapt attention.

"Now, why at Halloween? Well, I got news for you. It's not Halloween, not really. Halloween is where it is because the days are getting shorter, yeah? The nights are getting colder. The natural world is pulling away, withdrawing from us, and in times of change, the veil thins. But don't worry, don't worry!" Bernie boomed, his arms wide open. "It comes back. It always comes back. The cycle is eternal. Yeah? You know it is."

"I know it is," Ayla whispered. Melvin smiled at her.

"We are each separate. We are beings with our own lives. Our own little corner of the world," Bernie said. "But when the veil is thin, and you are here in this place, you can touch the eternal. You'll know, you'll know," he said with a cheerful little shimmy. "Oh, yes. You'll know that we are all eternal."

He threw his arms wide again, and lights flashed like reflections from a pool at night. Flickering and dancing green-blue ribbons of light—like tiny auroras—flashed and danced above our heads. We all, as one, looked up and stared.

"Daddy!" someone cried. "Dad, is that you?"

The park was filled with gasps, soft cries, and jubilant shouts.

"Wave at your loved ones through the doorway of life and death," Guru Bernie told them. "Know that they are always there and always with you, yeah?"

"Astra?" I stared in disbelief. Godfree Carrillo, a soldier I served with at the ministry, stared down at me through the haze of undulating aurora light. "Astra, do you remember me?"

"Of course I remember you, Godfree!" The guilt I'd shoved down so long ago bubbled up. Godfree was killed in action while trying to apprehend a particularly angry centaur. He was the first legionary I ever lost as Decanus. Losing anyone under your command is...life-changing. I took years to get over it. "Godfree, I'm so sorry I sent you out on that—"

"I did my duty," he said, cutting me off, his ghostly hand dismissing my regret. Godfree's handsome face was kind, sympathetic. He still looked so young. I guess no one ages in the great beyond. "The centaur had killed four people. Well, five if you count me," he said with a wide smile. "I don't regret anything. You have no reason to feel guilty. You were a good leader,

Astra. Fair. And you cared about us. I was proud to have served under you."

Suddenly, I was so choked up I could hardly breathe. My eyes filled with tears, and I quickly wiped them away. "That's nice of you to say, Godfree. But I'm not sure I deserved that. Especially not from you."

"You do. And Athena thought you might need to hear it."

I blinked. "Sorry?"

"I died a warrior's death, Decanus," Godfree told me, his voice suffused with pride. "Athena seeks out all warriors that sacrificed themselves in service to others, the thinking warriors that tried to resolve conflict." He smirked. "The crazy berserkers hang out with Ares." Then, suddenly, he looked behind him. "My turn's up, so I have to go. But I need to tell you something first."

I braced myself. "I'm ready."

He laughed. "That's kind of what I needed to tell you. That you are ready. But you're choosing not to be." Godfree leaned out a little bit, his torso slightly more visible, and looked around. "Hi, Astra's sisters!"

The three were staring, gobsmacked, at Godfree. They waved.

"Athena sent Archimedes to you because she

chose you to get her sister's power, but she wants you to know that doesn't mean the owl is only for you." He looked into my eyes. "You need to lead again, Astra. But before you can lead, you have to believe."

"Believe what?"

He stared at me, openmouthed, and laughed again. "You know what."

"You know, in the human world, there's freedom of religion, Godfree," I told him, crossing my arms. "I don't follow *anyone*. No worship, no following, no nothing. I tried that once, remember? Do you know what happened to Paranormopolis after you passed away? Do you know what the Witches' Council did?"

"I didn't say you had to follow," Godfree responded, his tone amused. "I just said you had to believe. It's only once you believe that you can start making real decisions about the type of leader you will be."

"Leader of what?"

"Being a leader is a state of being, Astra. Not a job." Godfree looked behind him again. "I got to go. If you come back next year, maybe I'll swing by." His eyes softened. "Remember me."

With that, Godfree faded into the aurora, and the ribbon above us moved on.

"Wow," Emma said, exhaling.

"I told you," Jason said, nodding. "Pretty amazing, huh?"

"What just happened?" Ayla asked, her face confused. "Like, he was here, but he wasn't here."

"Not all ghosts reside on this plane," Melvin explained to Ayla. "But on Halloween, when the veil is thin, they can peek through and speak to us even if they're somewhere else. We have an energy vortex or something in this park." Melvin shrugged. "It happens only for a few minutes, and then it's over."

"I want an energy vortex," Ami said, staring at the temporary aurora canopy. Several dozen shimmery, ethereal figures leaned down through them as if calling to someone at the bottom of a well.

"It's something we found, not something we created," Jason said. He turned to me, eyed my expression, and leaned in to whisper. "Are you okay? You look a little pale."

"I wasn't expecting that," I answered, then nodded. "But yeah, I'm fine." I yanked my hand out of his, which wasn't difficult because he was barely holding it. "Don't worry about me. I'm fine."

His dark eyes were filled with more emotions than I could count.

"Let's make our way toward the stage," Jason said, pointing. "Bernie has something for you to bring to your mom."

"I DON'T UNDERSTAND."

"It's the treaty we signed. I crossed out the deal to prevent going to visit each other's towns." Guru Bernie was literally standing in front of me, hands on my shoulders. "To tell you the truth, I've been thinking about tearing this thing up even before this," he said softly in my ear. "I'm dying to go to Parrot Paradise."

"We hope that your mother will be welcome here and that this can usher in a new era of cooperation and respect between the witches and us," Serena informed me formally. "We could not have freed our spectral community members without you, and we three realized that our insularity—"

"You mean intolerance," Ayla interrupted.

Serena paused and nodded. "It was not our intention, but you are correct. Our isolation and self-protection have fermented into intolerance.

It was never our intention to do so. Furthermore, it contradicts what we try to convey to our visitors: we have no beginning and no end. That we are one with everything and everyone."

"Even witches!" Guru Bernie said with a sing-song voice.

My sisters chuckled. The old man's joy really was infectious.

"On the political front, perhaps lifetime appointments are not the wisest way to go," Mayor Thornton said with a grimace. "To be fair, that started back when average lifespans were about forty-two. But still." She looked at Captain Harmon. "We got complacent. Our complacency nearly cost us everything."

"Edgar was not an evil man," Serena admitted. "But he was angry about his hearing loss, and when Jared and Robert healed him, they bought his allegiance and fed his anger." She looked down sadly. "We should have been there for him more than we were. Should have seen his anger and his pain."

"We hope that we can call on you," Mayor Thornton added. "Should we require witches in the future."

"Absolutely," I said, nodding.

And Cassandra would call on us again.

And again.
And we would call on them, too.
But that's a story for another time.

THANK YOU FOR READING!

I hope you enjoyed Heavy Meddle Magic. Please think about leaving a review! Astra, Archie and the whole Arden family continue their adventures in Book 5, Owl About Yule.

KEEP UP WITH LEANNE LEEDS

Thanks so much for reading! I hope you liked it! Want to keep up with me?

Visit leanneleeds.com to:

Find all my books...

Sign up for my newsletter...

Like me on Facebook...

Follow me on Twitter...

Follow me on Instagram...

Thanks again for reading!

Leanne Leeds

FIND A TYPO? LET US KNOW!

Typos happen. It's sad, but true.

Though we go over the manuscript multiple times, have editors, have beta readers, and advance readers it's inevitable that determined typos and mistakes sometimes find their way into a published book.

Did you find one? If you did, think about reporting it on leanneleeds.com so we can get it corrected.

ARTIFICIAL INTELLIGENCE STATEMENT

Portions of this book were created with the assistance of AI tools used for editing, proofreading, and refining the text. However, the ideas, storyline, characters, and overall creative vision remain my own original work.

While some aspects of the cover image were generated using AI tools, it was done so under my creative direction and curation.

I want to acknowledge the use of these technologies as part of my creative process, while affirming that the essence of this work comes from my own imagination and effort.

Leanne Leeds